IN SUCH DARK PLACES

IN SUCH
DARK PLACES

JOSEPH CALDWELL

ALYSON PUBLICATIONS INC.

BOSTON

The author wishes to thank

the MacDowell Colony, the Corporation of Yaddo,

and the Edward Albee Foundation

for providing the bright places in which

most of this novel was written

TO MY BROTHERS

AND MY SISTERS

1

"Mister! Mister! Take my picture!"

Just as Eugene focused on the young man dressed like a Roman soldier, a boy thrust his face in front of the camera and what Eugene got was a picture of a dirty nose. He wished the boy would let him alone. He'd come into the neighborhood to photograph a Holy Week street parade and not the nose, or any other part, of a thirteen-year-old boy.

Eugene was hung over, which was bad enough, but, beyond that, he didn't feel he belonged anywhere near anything remotely religious, even as a photographer. He was disgusted with himself, and had been for a long time. He'd counted on the parade to be a distraction, but it made him uneasy instead, more uneasy than he thought possible.

"Okay," Eugene said to the boy, trying to sound more tough than anguished, "I got your picture. Now stay out of my way." Stepping down into the gutter, he moved along the line of march to get clear of the boy and to try again for a picture of the soldier.

There were six soldiers behind the man carrying the cross, all of them flogging the pavement with whips made of clothesline. One in particular attracted Eugene. His name was Johnny. His whip rose higher than the others', flailed farther back, and was brought down onto the tail end of the cross itself with a crack that sounded sharp enough to split the wood. Even the Lenten hymn being shouted in Spanish by a chorus of determined women marching behind the soldiers failed to muffle the sound of the blows.

Por tu larga agonía,
Pequé, pequé, Dios mío,
Piedad, Señor, piedad,
Si grandes son mis culpas,
Más grande es tu bondad.

Eugene had studied Spanish in high school, but that was almost six years ago and only a vague sense of the words filtered through. He recognized *"agonía"* and knew there was a plea for "pity, Lord, pity." Or at least that's what he thought he heard.

Moving in closer, he focused on the soldier. He was about seventeen, shorter than Eugene, about five foot seven, with a hard-muscled body trimmed down, it seemed, by its own fierce energy. His hair was light brown and long enough to flop over his forehead with each stroke of the whip. The eyes, blue and bright, looked like two sporting animals, mischievous and free.

Eugene had first seen Johnny early that morning in an all-night diner on Avenue A, where he'd stopped after getting drunk—for the third time that week—in a bar on Second Street. It was thanks to Johnny that Eugene knew about the parade. Johnny and a friend whose name was Raimundo sat at a table in front of the one where Eugene was sloppily eating pancakes. Johnny faced Eugene directly and was trying to persuade Raimundo to be in the parade with him, telling him how handsome they would look in their Roman uniforms, how they could not disappoint Father Carusone (he had given it a full pronunciation: *Carusonay*), and that their costumes had been made by Reina and Reina was Raimundo's woman.

Raimundo, his back to Eugene, kept saying rather mournfully, "No, I don't think I want to do that." But Johnny had been dazzling in his persuasions. And when he saw Eugene watching him, he smiled and winked, not as a co-conspirator in the plot to get Raimundo into uniform, but in recognition of Eugene's appreciation of his performance. It was like a quick bow made to acknowledge applause, yet more intimate, a personal invitation to future performances, an invitation charged with the insolent promise that Eugene had seen nothing yet. There was more where all this came from. Plenty more.

Eugene moved back onto the sidewalk for a picture of all six soldiers. Raimundo, too, was in the parade after all, costumed in the uniform that his woman, Reina, had made. No longer a reluctant conscript, he seemed at times in competition with Johnny to see who could flog with greater enthusiasm. But where Johnny's eyes were mischievous, Raimundo's, slanted upward by the high cheekbones, were those of a confused pony, vulnerable and afraid, endangered and dangerous. Eugene took some pictures of Raimundo too, then changed the lens for a closer view of Johnny. He was still hung over, but at least his hands were steady.

Johnny's golden armor, his breastplate and helmet, was gilded *papier-mâché*, and his tunic was scarlet-dyed burlap. A crest of red crepe paper crowned the helmet, a bold attempt at imperial glory. Eugene snapped the shutter.

Again the boy had stepped in front of the camera. "Mister! Take my picture!"

Eugene wanted to kill him, but experience had taught him never to show anger when working in the streets. Try for cooperation, or at least distraction. "You're going to miss the parade!" he shouted over the women's song.

"I saw it all last year," yelled the boy. "They're going to crucify him across from the A&P. What kind of a camera is that?"

"Ask me later."

"Give me a dollar and I'll help." The boy's tone surprised Eugene. This was not extortion but an honest offer.

"I don't have a dollar."

"Then take my picture."

"I'm trying to take pictures of the parade."

"It's not a parade. It's a procession."

"How far is the A&P?"

"Two blocks down, one right."

Eugene moved closer to the boy so he wouldn't have to keep shouting. "If I give you a dollar, will you go save me a place at the A&P?"

"Can't I help here?"

"I need a place saved. Okay?"

"Yeah. I guess so."

Eugene gave him a dollar, careful not to pull out the other two he had in his pocket. He didn't want to waste time haggling over the price. The boy took the money and stayed right where he was.

Eugene ran up ahead as much to get away from him as to take pictures of the chorus.

Por tu costado abierto,
Pequé, pequé, Dios mío,
Piedad, Señor, piedad,
Si grandes son mis culpas,
Más grande es tu bondad.

"If great are my sins, more great is your goodness" was the best Eugene could come up with.

Oblivious to anything but their hymn, the women stepped brightly along, the wind lifting their blue silken skirts to show ankle socks or panty hose. He thought of them as the sorrowing Daughters of Jerusalem, but if their song was meant to be a dirge, they had forgotten. One plump lady, her face uplifted, her golden headband fallen down over one eye, raised her voice so that her song should be heard on the mountain and on the plain. The others took inspiration from her and shouted out the words as if to warn all within hearing that their grief was great and that it defied consolation.

How different all this was from the Stations of the Cross at Holy Trinity back in Atlantis, Iowa. There they looked at sculpted plaques spaced between the stained-glass windows and sang softly, "O Sacred Head Surrounded." There they gently prayed, genuflected, meditated, prayed again, and sang some more. The priest and the acolytes did all the walking, and that was only up one aisle and down the other.

> *Por tu madre afligida,*
> *Pequé, pequé, Dios mío,*
> *Piedad, Señor, piedad,*
> *Si grandes son mis culpas,*
> *Más grande es tu bondad.*

"For your afflicted mother, guilty, guilty, my God . . ."

Passing in front of him now were those loyal people of the parish content to march as mere civilians, the

Citizens, he supposed, of Jerusalem. They seemed to him the most absurd of all. With no specific assignment, no singing, no whipping, they walked in self-conscious disarray, either staring straight ahead or talking to each other out of embarrassment at making such a spectacle of themselves. Their clothes were their best; one woman even wore a full-length coat of indeterminate fur, in spite of the spring weather.

Then, at the rag end of the ranks, a man with grizzled, close-cropped hair shuffled along, his rosary beads whispering through his fingers as his lips nibbled the air to form the words. He was wearing a brown and black herringbone suit several sizes too large, and his heavy-crusted shoes looked as though he had come a long way through dirt and through mud. Eugene wondered if it was the Joyful, Glorious, or Sorrowful Mysteries that made the man smile as he walked the road to Calvary.

He took the picture, then turned abruptly away and looked far down the block. There was the man in purple carrying the cross, a priest in billowing alb at his side. That would be Father Carusone. He was wearing dark-rimmed glasses and Eugene immediately decided they made the priest look foolish. In fact, he encouraged himself to see the entire parade as something ridiculous. That would be the approach his pictures would take.

He was there, after all, not just because of his attraction to Johnny but for legitimate artistic reasons. He could get a good series out of the parade, which, in turn, might give some momentum to his halted career. Maybe a magazine sale, or a show at a decent gallery, maybe even a book. Fantasies? Well, even so, that's why he was there. Not, he told himself, just because of Johnny.

By adjusting the lens, Eugene was able to include the singing Daughters of Jerusalem as well as the Citizens of the City, except for the straggling man with the rosary. He also got the spectators along the sidewalk and in the tenements up to the second floor. One woman leaned out her window waving, applauding, shouting, *"Viva! Viva el Cristo Rey! Viva el Cristo!"* Her plump breasts and long kinky hair, serrated like the teeth of a lumberman's saw, made Eugene think of Helen. And he'd hoped not to think of her the entire day. He loathed her. He didn't loathe her. He loathed himself. He didn't loathe himself.

"Viva! Viva el Cristo Rey!"

To move, to move anywhere, to get away, he half ran to the back end of the parade, or procession, or whatever it was called. He'd get some pictures from there.

About twenty feet behind the last praying pilgrim, high on a sleek bay mare, a helmeted policeman rode uneasy in the saddle, barely able to rein the beast to a skittish prance. It kept jerking its head to the side, to the left, as though wanting to bear its rider in another direction entirely, away from the mob huddled in its path.

Eugene raised the camera. He caught the chanting, scourging throng down the street, with the policeman and the horse centered in the foreground. And he saw now what made the animal so reluctant. The parade seemed like anything but a procession to the Holy Mountain. It was a rabble marching on to the palace of Pilate himself, ready to cry out for vengeance, for justice, and for blood.

Eugene clicked the camera to shut the vision out.

Por tu pasión y muerte,
Pequé, pequé, Dios mío,
Piedad, señor, piedad,
Si grandes son mis culpas,
Más grande es tu bondad.

"For your passion and death . . . pity, Lord, pity . . ."
From a tenement stoop he focused on the man with the cross. Sweat was coursing down his face and neck, dampening the wood where it lay in the notch of his shoulder. His eyes looked down at the ground as though he had been condemned to number each and every stone for a later accounting. The robe he wore was mottled and streaked with dark wet stains, dyeing the royal purple almost black. Eugene saw that it was actually a worn flannel bathrobe, stitched up the front and trimmed with cheap gold braid. He stared at the bowed head, then out over the entire length of the parade.

It was no use. What he saw now was not ridiculous but something totally beautiful. It was futile to try to deny it.

Eugene heard the women's shouted song as a gallant cry in the face of irremediable loss, and Father Carusone's black-rimmed glasses were touching, they were so out of place. The man with the rosary shuffled by, still nibbling the air, still smiling, and never had the phrase "the last shall be first" seemed to Eugene more right and just.

The marching people seemed now—glasses, bathrobe, crusted shoes, and all—they seemed to him surely a pilgrim people marching, not to the A&P or even toward their Calvary, but toward the gates of heaven itself, for this was the only way to enter: a procession of fools, inadequate and unashamed.

He held his breath, then let go, slowly. A sudden sorrow had taken hold of him. He almost wished that he could march with them, that he could be part of their beauty, that with them he would be one of the true inheritors of the earth.

But, he sternly reminded himself, he could never be one with these people, any more than he could be one with the people at Holy Trinity back in Atlantis. Nor, he told himself, did he want to be. He was an outsider, even by profession. He did not participate. He took pictures.

He jumped down the steps and moved quickly up the block, well ahead of the procession. Two policemen on motorcycles growled toward him like a surly honor guard making way for the man with the cross. He shot from an angle that placed one cyclist's immobile face right next to the bowed and sweaty head. He hated melodrama, but it would sell.

───────────

Por tus tres duros clavos,
Pequé, pequé, Dios mío,
Piedad, Señor, piedad,
Si grandes son mis culpas,
Más grande es tu bondad.

"For your three sharp nails . . . more great is your goodness . . ."

Eugene watched as Johnny came closer. He saw the armored body arch backward, drawn by the rising whip. He saw the downward pitch and heard the cry of triumph as each blow landed.

Taking no pictures, simply watching, Eugene imagined himself the focus of all that thrashing power, imagined having it spend itself on him, so that finally the soldier would be helpless, conquered, and in need of comfort, comfort Eugene might or might not give. He liked the moment of power, of choice.

"You were going to take my picture!"

The shout was muffled, and Eugene turned to see where it came from. The boy was standing next to him, the neck of his T-shirt stretched up over his nose like a bandit's mask.

"You were going to take my picture!" He let the T-shirt drop as though to scare Eugene with the revelation of his true identity. Eugene ignored him and turned again toward the street. He watched Johnny rear back, his hair beneath his helmet fly out like the mane of a colt, then fall forward with the downstroke. Johnny seemed to be smiling. Eugene took his picture.

"You promised you'd take it if I saved you a place."

Eugene looked at the boy, annoyed, then walked ahead to keep up with the soldiers. The boy followed, tugging on the camera pouch slung from Eugene's shoulder.

"Come on. You promised."

"I didn't promise. I gave you a dollar."

"How about if I give *you* a dollar? Then will you take my picture?"

"I don't want a dollar."

"Then take it for a quarter."

Eugene stopped and pivoted toward the boy. He brought the camera up and clicked the shutter. "There! I took your picture."

"I wasn't ready!"

"You wanted me to take your picture and I took your picture." He took another.

"Wait, I told you." The boy brought his fist back as though he were going to punch him. Eugene clicked the shutter again.

"All right, take it then! Only I'm not going to give you the quarter!" The boy made a face, a screwed-up scowl with a jutting jaw. Then with his thumbs he stretched his mouth wide. His tongue hung out, wagging itself from side to side.

Eugene continued to take pictures.

Finally the boy stopped and just stood there, his repertory exhausted. What Eugene saw now was a scrawny kid in a dirty tan jacket with an even dirtier

T-shirt underneath. His hair was chestnut brown and fell over the right side of his forehead. There was a small scar that lay like a worm track just below his right eye, running from the cheekbone toward his ear. The ears themselves were not particularly large, but they stuck out as though they had been used to pull the boy free from his mother's womb, out into the world. His expression, even now, seemed to ask why he had been treated in this rough and mocking way.

Turning away from the camera, the boy stared down at the sidewalk as though ashamed of letting Eugene see his unguarded face. He plunged his fists into his jacket pockets, then raised his head with a defiant sniff. "The place I saved is on top of Gregory's delivery cart. Only you got to give me another dollar."

Eugene gave him the dollar. "Now take me to where it is." He was pleased that his voice sounded gruff.

A crowd was collecting in the lot across from the A&P when they got there. The boy brought Eugene to a parked delivery cart in front of the store. He banged on its lid to demonstrate its sturdiness and prove that Eugene was getting his money's worth. "You stand up there and you'll see everything. Go on. It's all right. I got you permission especially."

Eugene climbed up and looked into the lot across the street. An imposing mound of rubble stood at its center, its foundation the gutted carcass of a Volkswagen. Thrown together were mattresses, bureau drawers, smashed television sets, metal cabinets dented beyond use, a toilet bowl, a few rubber tires, and assorted parts from the cannibalized Volkswagen. Idle garbage filled in the open spaces.

"They do it on top of all that?" Eugene asked.

"He stands up there and they put the cross behind him and he holds his arms open wide. Then Father says something about how people are getting crucified all the time right here in the neighborhood and everybody says a prayer and then we all get to sing."

The motorcycles droned closer, and Eugene jumped down from the cart and moved quickly past the man with the cross to get just a few more pictures of Johnny. The women's song was rising in fervor and the soldiers, too, seemed to have found new energy as they approached the moment of crucifixion. Johnny, however, no longer seemed to be concentrating on the man with the cross. He was still lashing down with his whip, but mostly, Eugene thought, to goad Raimundo into flailing harder. Each time Raimundo hit the pavement or the cross, Johnny would let out a long "aaagh," almost in mockery of Raimundo's seriousness. Obviously, to Johnny the procession had become a joke, the same joke Eugene kept trying to see. But to Raimundo it was anything but. He stared fixedly at the cross, flogging it mercilessly, as if determined to subdue some threatening living thing.

When Eugene looked more closely, he saw that the sweat trickling down Raimundo's cheeks was not sweat at all but tears. He stared a moment, then began to take pictures.

"You want me to carry the pouch, so you can work better?"

Without taking the camera from his eye, Eugene flapped his elbow to shake off the boy's touch. "It's got my other camera," he said. "I'm going to need it."

Raimundo wiped away the tears with the back of his left hand, not missing a single stroke of the whip. As Eugene watched through the lens, he saw the face contort and the lips begin to tremble. Finally Raimundo started to sob. His shoulders heaved. No longer marching, standing still, he let the whip fall limp at his side and brought his other hand up to cover his face. Johnny stayed close by, watching, but with no more than a mildly amused curiosity.

The women, singing away for all they were worth, came up from behind and bumped into them. Still singing, they stopped, first to stare and then to look helplessly at each other. Now the second and third rows collided with the women surrounding the weeping soldier and the singing trailed off. Questions were being asked in Spanish and in English and comfort offered. But Raimundo would not take his hand from his face or check his tears.

Eugene went right on taking pictures.

Gradually, the other soldiers became aware that, without the singing, they could hear their own grunts. Each continued his flailings, but turned his head toward the mob gathering behind. One of the soldiers nicked the priest's arm. The priest ignored it until it happened the third time. Then he, too, looked back. The soldiers, confused, stopped their scourging altogether and started toward the crowd around Raimundo. The priest followed.

The man carrying the cross, now aware that he was unattended, stopped and turned. The rabble, the Citizens of Jerusalem, joined by some of the spectators, had grouped around the soldier. As he stood sobbing, refusing all comfort, Eugene took picture after picture, devouring as many details as he could: Father Carusone gently touching Raimundo's arm; a child sucking her thumb, looking up as though she had never before seen a man cry; the puzzled arrival of the man with the cross.

Raimundo took his hand from his face. He tried to speak, but his lips moved soundlessly. Slowly he moved his head from side to side, the tears dripping freely from his chin, raising welts on his golden armor.

He looked toward Eugene but without seeing him. Eugene lowered the camera as if in respect. The soldier's face was wet and streaked with dirt. His lips were parched in spite of the thick threads of mucus and saliva that stretched and snapped as he tried to speak. The dark eyes were half shut and the lower lashes, black and swollen, curled down, touching the cheek, heavy with tears. So he wouldn't startle him, or interrupt his agony, Eugene raised the camera very slowly. But he was *too* slow. Raimundo hid his face again, mumbling something in Spanish that Eugene couldn't understand.

"What's he saying?" Eugene whispered to anyone who might know.

"He's saying he's sorry." It was the boy who answered.

Eugene gave him a quick impatient glance, then looked again at Raimundo. "Sorry about what?"

"Nothing. Just he's sorry."

Eugene moved to the edge of the crowd to get a larger view. When he turned back, there was a stirring at the center. The stirring quickened, accompanied by a growing murmur. Suddenly Raimundo burst through, snatched up the cross where the man had laid it, and hauled it about ten feet. He shouted back at the mob.

"What's he saying?"

The boy answered, "He didn't mean to do it."

"Didn't mean to do what?"

"Nothing. Just he didn't mean to do it."

The crowd, recovering from its surprise, moved ominously toward the soldier, led by the man who had been carrying the cross. But when the man tried to retrieve his property, Raimundo shoved him away. Before the priest could get to them, they were pushing each other and tugging at the cross. The man fell against an advancing Citizen, who angrily thrust him back toward Raimundo. Now the man gave a quick push at those nearest him, a woman with a child and Johnny. By the time he returned to his quarrel with Raimundo (who had, by now, placed the cross on his own shoulder), those who had been pushed were pushing the man, Johnny, and each other as well.

The cross was knocked from Raimundo's back and

he retaliated by punching Johnny, who had merely been shoving a Daughter of Jerusalem, not him or his cross.

The Daughters, too, were shoving now and the women with children started to move cautiously away. A warning, whinnying sound came from the horse as the policeman struggled to keep it under control. The lead singer took up her song but stopped when knocked on the side of the head by a soldier taking a swing at a spectator. The priest kept fighting his way through, calling out words Eugene could not hear. Then a thrown bottle shattered.

Terrified, the horse reared up with a bleating, snorting cry. The rider tried to rein it back, but it plunged down into the crowd, trampling and scattering as it reared and plunged again.

The mob grabbed garbage from the cans in front of the tenements and pelted the panicked horse and its rider as well. The two policemen abandoned their motorcycles and waded into the melee, their clubs beating a path as they went.

Clutching the camera with both hands, Eugene moved in closer, getting picture after picture. A gallery show was almost a certainty, he told himself, and publication of the series a good possibility. There might also be a newspaper sale that evening when it was all over. He savored every bit of it.

Then a shriek pierced his left ear. Eugene turned and saw a woman dragging a little girl, who was being knocked first one way and then the other by the knees and feet around her. The child's dress was ripped. Her eyes darted from knee to knee in the quick glances of an animal at bay.

Letting the camera fall loose on its strap, Eugene reached down and swooped the child up. The woman screamed and beat him on the back with her fists.

"Let me get her out of here before she gets killed!" he yelled. But the woman either didn't hear or didn't understand.

He held the girl against him and struggled toward the sidewalk. Spreading one of his huge farm-boy hands over her back, he spanned it like an extra set of ribs, providing protection against the blows of elbows and fists. With the other he shielded her head, making sure that his thumb and the heel of his hand touched almost tenderly along the soft cheek.

The woman clutched at Eugene's hair, then dug her nails into the back of his neck.

"Stop! I'm trying to help!" He turned toward her and she aimed for his eyes. Eugene pulled his head away. A rock glanced off his shoulder.

Bending over the child, he tried a billy-goat charge, but the mother held fast to the back of his jacket, weeping and pleading, and he had to pull her along.

Clear of the mob, Eugene sat the little girl down on a stoop. Safe now, she began to cry. He bent over to hold her again, to comfort and reassure her, but he felt the woman's fists pummel his back. When he turned to explain, she aimed again at his eyes.

To escape, Eugene forced his way back into the riot, his only concession to his upbringing being that he helped a woman up after knocking her down. Once he stumbled over the forgotten cross. Then he fell and the camera was almost trampled, but he managed to raise himself by grabbing the sleeve of the full-length fur coat and hoisting himself up. The fur felt like pig bristle.

He took one more picture, then tried to flick the advance. It locked. He was out of film.

Quickly he changed to the backup camera in his pouch. A shower of coffee grounds and eggshells spewed down from a broken garbage bag flying overhead.

The boy, he saw, was at his side, punching and kicking wherever his services seemed needed most. "Watch out for blades," he yelled. At the words, Eugene realized he had seen a glint of steel, once on the pavement and twice flashing in the crowd, but he kept moving, the camera clicking away.

Suddenly, above the shouts and cries, he heard the fall of shattering glass. One of the A&P windows. Sirens were coming closer. The raw wail seemed to drive the rioters to an even greater frenzy.

The backup camera ran out: he remembered taking almost a whole roll in the park the day before. There was film in the pouch for the first camera, the Nikon, but he'd have to get clear before he could make the change. Another window crashed, this time followed by screams for help.

Eugene fought his way to the curb, but when he grabbed down into the pouch, the Nikon wasn't there. He looked around. The boy, too, was gone.

Eugene jumped to the top of the delivery cart. He couldn't see the boy, either in or out of the mob. More sirens sounded. Soldiers, Citizens, spectators, and some of the Daughters of Jerusalem now invaded the empty lot. The mound was dismantled, its contents thrown at the rioters in the street. The carcass of the Volkswagen was rolled out onto the sidewalk and a metal cabinet was flung clattering and crumpling against it.

Eugene looked out over the street. He thought he saw the scarlet crest of Johnny's helmet, now a flashing cock's comb. But it wasn't Johnny, it was Raimundo. Johnny was nowhere in sight, nor was the boy.

Trash, tin cans, bottles, stones, everything came flying from the lot. A chunk of brick crashed against the cart. Eugene jumped down and picked it up. The boy had stolen the camera with most of the pictures in it. He hurled the rock high into the mob. A stone from Golgotha answered, then a headlight from the Volkswagen.

He ducked them both and ran toward the corner. He had to find the boy before he got too far.

Furious, he kicked a brown paper bag that lay in his path, and hurt his foot on the bottle inside. He yelled more in rage than in pain, but no one heard.

2

Eugene rang the rectory bell, stamping his feet on the step as though they were cold. In an effort to calm his impatience, he read three times a sign nailed to the rectory door. It was printed with colored crayons and invited everyone, in Spanish and in English, to a sunrise Mass at Tenth Street and the East River at five o'clock Easter morning. The sun decorating the sign had more than twice the colors of the rainbow itself and was smiling a jolly, if one-lipped, smile.

Wondering what its smile would be if it could see what had happened in front of the A&P, Eugene rang the bell again. When he'd read the sign twice more and still no one answered, he walked in.

He had already ranged through all the streets in the

neighborhood looking and asking for the boy, but he'd gotten nowhere. The first person he'd talked to was a woman in a loose cotton house dress and bedroom slippers who had come up to him just as he turned the corner from the A&P. She had looked at him with terror and asked something in Spanish. He answered by asking, "Did you see a kid with a camera?"

The woman repeated her question, begging for an answer, so Eugene simply said, "Around the corner at the A&P." She drew in a quick breath, brought her fingers to her cheek, and waddled rapidly toward the corner, the back ends of her worn slippers slapping against her bare heels. Eugene heard her call, "John-neee! John-neee!"

"Wait! Don't go there. He'll be all right," Eugene yelled after her. He didn't know if she was calling the Johnny he knew, but it would be better if she didn't see what was happening. "Wait for him here. He'll be right home." A police car raced by, lights flashing, its siren bellowing with the heaving, retching sound of a bull trying to vomit. The woman hadn't listened or hadn't heard. She had already turned the corner.

When he had asked a man sitting on a kitchen chair in the middle of the sidewalk who looked as though he were guarding his garbage cans, the man stopped trying to force up some phlegm long enough to tell Eugene to look for the boy in the park, in Tompkins Square.

In the park, he saw a black man asleep on a bench with a white cat sitting on his stomach, swishing its tail, fanning the man's face. Eugene had once thought of doing a photographic series of people asleep in public places, but the idea had no force for him at the moment. And besides, he had no camera with film in it.

Leaving the park, he saw Father Carusone coming down Avenue B toward the church just across the street. The priest's white robe was rolled up under one arm and he was wearing plain black pants and a sleeveless argyle sweater over a blue sports shirt. He was helping a limping man, while a woman trailed two steps behind, gesturing and talking wildly. They entered the rectory next to the church, and Eugene crossed the street to follow. Someone there must know where he could find the boy and get the camera back. The fact that the lost film contained most of his pictures of Johnny was no small contribution to the urgency he felt.

The sparely furnished room at the front of the rectory was in effect a busy clinic or the emergency room of a hospital. An ample, efficient-looking woman in a snug black dress was applying iodine to the gash on a man's leg; a Daughter of Jerusalem had a basin of water and was washing the bloodied cheek of a young girl in dungarees. The woman in the full-length fur coat was patting the girl's hand and sobbing. A man with a bloodied handkerchief pressed to the top of his skull was speaking furiously in Spanish to another man, who was holding his right arm as rigid and close to his side as possible. A phone was ringing in the next room. The limping man was pulling off his shoe to show the priest his foot. High above the general noise, a long-drawn wail of "aiyee, aiyee, aiyee" came from the man getting the iodine. It sounded more like a religious incantation than a cry of pain.

The woman in the fur coat, still sobbing, came up to Eugene and asked him a question in Spanish. Eugene could only look at her in confusion. He should have studied harder. He should have studied, period.

The priest, still examining the man's foot, said, "She wants to know where you're hurt."

The woman nodded her head and repeated what she'd said before. Eugene felt the claw marks on his neck, but there was no blood. Looking down, however, he saw that his pants were ripped above the left knee and that the right sleeve of his jacket had been slashed in two places. There was blood of no remembered origin on his left sleeve, and some had run down onto his hand. He wiped it on his pants, but it was too dried to come off. "Nowhere," he answered.

"Madeleine," said Father Carusone, "could you get the phone?"

The woman in the black dress handed the man whose wound she'd been dressing a strip of cloth for a bandage and went into the next room.

Eugene walked over to the priest, who was very gently peeling a filthy and sweat-soaked sock off the man's foot. "Pardon me, Father, but I was taking some pictures of your procession and—"

The priest stood up. "Wash his foot."

"What?"

"He won't go to the hospital because it's dirty. Get it as clean as you can without hurting him."

Eugene shook his head. "No, I'm just here looking for my camera. I think some kid, dirty T-shirt, tan jacket..."

Madeleine came back into the room. "Father Carusone?" She, too, pronounced the name *Carusonay.*

"Just wash his foot," said the priest as he left the room.

Next to the man with the foot, a girl with a basin of water was cleaning the scraped knee of a woman who kept fingering the rip in her stocking, whimpering, as though the frayed threads were the real source of her pain.

Eugene turned to the girl. "Did you see a kid with a camera coming away from the procession?"

"How bad was he hurt?" asked the girl.

"He wasn't hurt at all. He just swiped my camera, is all."

"I don't think I saw him." She offered Eugene a wet washcloth. Ignoring it, he asked the room in general if anyone had seen a boy, about thirteen, dirty T-shirt, gray corduroy pants, small scar on his cheek, with a camera; but the only response he got was from the man whose leg Madeleine was bandaging. "Better ask Father."

When Eugene turned to the man with the foot to ask his help, he recognized him as the pilgrim who had been praying the rosary. "You didn't see a kid—"

"He's Rumanian," interrupted the girl, putting the washcloth in Eugene's hand. "Mr. Economu." Mr. Economu smiled a coffee-stained smile which included one dull gold tooth, as if that confirmed his Rumanian origin. He held out his foot.

Eugene turned around to see if the priest had come back into the room. He wanted to find out what he could about the boy and go. He did not want to wash anyone's foot. But Father Carusone wasn't there. The sobbing woman in the fur coat slowly shook her head as if to indicate that hope for all good things had fled the world.

Eugene looked down at the outstretched foot. He might as well wash it while he waited for the priest. It was beginning to swell and turn blue. Its stench was like something rotting at the bottom of a well. There was no way to tell where the mealy dirt ended and the callused flesh began.

Eugene wrapped the camera pouch in his jacket and shoved it under the chair, then squatted down to roll back the man's pants leg and the soiled long underwear beneath it. He soaped the rag, took hold of the leg very carefully, and began to scrub the foot.

With a great shout the man jerked his leg up. Then the shout became a laugh, a high "hee-hee-hee" sound. When it stopped, Eugene brought the foot down and forward and touched it again with the rag, only this time higher up, near the ankle. The man made quick, repeated, half-sung sounds, alternating between a low howl and the high "hee-hee-hee." As Eugene moved the rag down closer to the foot itself, the man, in reflex, jerked his leg up again, gasping with pain and giggling helplessly. He looked at Eugene, laughed outright, three loud laughs, then took the calf of the leg between his two hands and held the foot toward Eugene as though offering it for his admiration. He said something Eugene interpreted as permission to try again.

After soaping the rag thoroughly, he sloshed it onto the man's foot and began, very lightly, to scrub.

Eugene was no longer in the rectory room but in the porcelain-tiled washroom of a men's shelter just off the Bowery. A man was lying back in an enormous white tub holding up his leg and Eugene was washing his toes. It was a year ago last fall. A friend of his, Lester, had told him about the shelter, suggesting it as a subject worth photographing for a series.

Eugene liked the idea. Real live human degradation, big-city style, was foreign to him still and the opportunity to see it firsthand excited him. After calling his boss at the moving company where he worked part-time, and telling him he had to go back to Iowa for two weeks, a family emergency, he presented himself to the people at the shelter as a volunteer. His plan was to work as one of them and then, once he was accepted and trusted, to mention taking the pictures. He was certain they wouldn't refuse. It should take him less than the two weeks he had free.

An old woman with a humped back and the softest voice he had ever heard asked him if he would mind washing some walls and scrubbing some floors. It wasn't what Eugene had in mind, but he moved in that night and began scrubbing floors in the morning.

Three days later, he was given kitchen duty, which was a little less lonesome. He had to get up earlier in the morning, but he didn't mind. On the farm he'd had to get up just as early.

Although most of the men who came to the shelter limited their talk to either bragging or whining, as opposed to the stories of human woe Eugene had hoped to hear, he managed to enjoy the work and the people he was working with, the consumptive cook, the hump-backed woman, and a whey-faced young man who always wore a suit, wrinkled and too large. He liked them all. He even liked himself.

He hadn't forgotten about the pictures, but he was feeling too good to want anything to intrude just yet. He would know when the right moment had come.

At the end of the week, he was assigned an additional job, to give new arrivals a Cuprex bath, a bath in chemicals to delouse them. Eugene had to scrub the men himself, every inch, to make sure they didn't just wet themselves in the chemicals and come out as infested as when they went in.

This assignment was not such a good idea. Even though he worked himself to exhaustion every day, he was becoming more and more fevered, more and more obsessively sexual. Even the whey-faced young man in the oversized wrinkled suit had begun to look pretty good to him. He was determined, however, to keep sex out of the entire enterprise.

He threw himself into the work with a fury that

amused and troubled his colleagues. When he scrubbed the kitchen floor on his knees, the woman with the humped back had laughed at him, but softly, gently.

Two days later, three men who had come to the shelter, derelicts just out of the hospital, one with half his teeth missing, began to seem quite handsome to Eugene. The next day, unbidden, he washed the dormitory walls and considered doing the windows, inside and out.

On the night of the tenth day, however, a young man came in off the Bowery asking shelter. Eugene gave him the much needed Cuprex bath, scrubbing as hard as he could, especially the feet, even between the toes. But when he washed his back, the young man began to have an erection. Eugene ignored it and even began to whistle. But while he was drying the man's back he could help himself no longer.

Handing the man the towel, he told him to finish drying himself and to get dressed in the clean clothes that had been set out for him. Eugene then went to the door. He even got it open, but only a few inches. Closing it again, he went back to the man. After a shrug indicating "Why not," the man put the palms of both hands on Eugene's shoulders and, with a pressure that was firm but not aggressive, forced him down onto his knees in front of him.

Afterwards, the man, still saying nothing, simply smiled a rather mocking smile, dressed, and left the room. Eugene scrubbed the tub, put the towel into the laundry, and left the shelter without saying goodbye to the humpbacked woman, the whey-faced young man, or the consumptive cook, and without having taken a single picture.

Somewhere around this time, Eugene stopped going to Mass and to the Sacraments, not as a conscious decision, but out of perplexity. He no longer had any sense of where he stood among men and God, and the placement bureau within him seemed to have shut down without notice.

Now he continued to slosh away at Mr. Economu's foot, careful not to apply too much pressure. He could see not only the terrible swelling but a hard dry bulb growing out of the side of the foot like an incipient toe. The toes themselves were twisted and pinched together as though they'd been squabbling among themselves and got stuck that way. The sole of the foot was like a rasp. Yet when Eugene touched the rag there, the leg slipped from the man's hold and plunged into the basin. The wash water splashed up onto Eugene's face, onto his lips, into his eyes.

The man's body became rigid and he sucked in the air in short fast spasms. Eugene looked up. The man's eyes were wide more with horror than with pain. Slowly he relaxed, and Eugene reached cautiously for the foot. The man's hand, rougher and more callused than the sole of his foot, took Eugene under the chin and lifted up his face. The man was looking at him with such profound sorrow that Eugene tried to turn away.

Gently, the man brushed the splashed drops of water from Eugene's face as if they were tears, then withdrew his foot from the basin and looked away, ashamed.

"I'm almost through," Eugene said, trying to sound encouraging. "Let me finish, okay?"

The man said nothing but, without looking directly at Eugene, locked the leg again between his hands and held out the foot to be washed. While Eugene scrubbed, the man tried not to laugh, even when he was being washed between the toes.

The girl finished cleaning the woman's knee and looked over to see how Eugene was doing. "It's going to be so shining," she said, smiling.

"You think so?" Eugene asked. He was very eager now to get it clean.

"Look at it, how different it is already," said the girl.

Eugene smiled gratefully, then remembered that he had not come to wash a foot. "You didn't see a boy in a tan jacket at all?" he asked. "Even without a camera? You don't know who he is or where he lives? I really need to get my camera back. It's my whole work and everything."

"He was wearing a tan jacket?" The girl, sounding as though she was trying to decide whether or not she wanted to remember, looked out the window at the park across the street.

"Dirty T-shirt, small scar here on the cheek."

The girl looked back at him, but before she could say anything, a door slammed and he heard angry voices in the hallway. The shouts got louder, until finally one of the soldiers was brought into the room, held firmly between two older men. Dried blood streaked his face and he was waving a clenched fist, shouting and struggling to get free. "Let me fight! Let me fight!"

Father Carusone appeared in the doorway. "Gregory, shut up." The voice was a little too quiet and too high-pitched for command, but the soldier and the men turned toward the priest. Father Carusone stood there trying to clear his throat so he could bring his voice back under control.

So this was Gregory. (Eugene did not think now was the time to thank him for the use of the delivery cart.) The two men let him go at the priest's instruction, and the youth sank down and squatted in a corner of the room. He clutched the top of his head, covering his face with his arms as though to hide, not his wounds, but his shame. "Why don't you let me fight?"

The priest cleared his throat and, testing it, said, "Let Nilda . . ." He cleared his throat again and said more firmly, "Let Nilda wash your face, so we can see where you're hurt." He turned to Eugene. "Finish his foot. We have to go to the hospital."

Madeleine stopped bandaging the man's leg. "What did they say about Johnny?"

"Stabbed. He was dead when they got him to the hospital."

The woman in the fur coat stopped sobbing. Eugene slowly pulled the washcloth away from the foot but didn't turn around. Everything became silent except for the man's cry of "aiyee, aiyee, aiyee," but that was more plaintive now and hushed.

Gregory leaned his head back against the wall and closed his eyes. Nilda knelt in front of him, reached up with a wet cloth, and began to dab the streaks on his face. He made no sound, gave no protest.

The priest looked at the foot. "Finish, so we can go."

It confused Eugene that Johnny should be dead, and before he had time to decide how he really felt, he knew that he was, above all, pleased. If someone had to be killed that day, it pleased him that it was someone he knew, someone who meant something to him, even though they had never actually met. Now Eugene himself was a part of the drama. It made him feel included and important. The event involved him. He bent over the foot and squeezed a fully soaked rag over it to rinse the soap away.

What if there was a picture of the murder in the stolen camera? He wanted to resist thinking of his own profit, but what the picture—or pictures!—could mean to his series was too incredible to ignore.

He kept rinsing Mr. Economu's foot, one squeezed rag after another. The lost film—it could even redeem him from the calamity of last fall, a show of sorts in a cheesy storefront tucked away on Broome Street. Oblivion, except for one review in a neighborhood newspaper: "Superficial, inverted, private to the point of non-existence." That same week, he got arrested for having sex with his cab driver after getting drunk up-town. A squad car had pulled alongside to see if any-thing was wrong. Ten days, sentence suspended.

The way Eugene had been feeling since, he'd be working the rest of his life, off and on, for the same crummy non-union moving company (Prime Movers, Greenwich Village, U.S.A.), with time out to do a little carpentry for extra money. But the lost film . . .

Eugene turned to Father Carusone, wondering if it would still be possible, under the circumstances, to ask about the camera and the boy. The priest was guiding toward the hallway door the man holding the handker-chief to his head, and Madeleine was helping the one who kept his arm clutched close to his side.

"Father?"

"Finish the foot," the priest said, without looking at him.

The foot was clean, the lumpy blue veins visible among the pale brown blotches that covered its top like large faded freckles. The tight skin of the incipient toe glistened. Water dripped onto the knee of Eugene's pants as he stayed hunched down, looking at the foot. He remembered the woman in the loose house dress and the worn slippers. "John-neee . . . John-neee," she had cried. Eugene saw the slippers slapping up against her bare heels.

He looked around for a towel or a rag to dry the foot but saw nothing. He reached into his back pocket, pulled out a clean handkerchief, and flapped it open.

"His name is David. David Stokes. He lives on Fifth

Street near Avenue B, over the Polish meat market."
Nilda, washing the soldier's face, was telling Eugene
what he needed to know to find the boy.

"Thanks. I mean . . . thank you . . ."

Eugene dried the foot. The man brought it up to
give it a closer look, then indicated to Eugene that it
wasn't dry enough between the toes. Eugene dried between them and the man giggled.

"Take him out to the car," Eugene heard the priest
say. Father Carusone was examining Gregory's head for
cuts, but Eugene knew he was talking about Mr.
Economu. He tossed the used handkerchief under the
chair. Bunching his jacket closer around the pouch, he
stood up, tucking the wadded roll under his left arm.
With his right hand, he helped Mr. Economu up, then
placed the man's arm around his shoulders to support
him so that he wouldn't touch the floor with his fresh
clean foot.

In the hallway, Father Carusone opened the outside
door and stood back to let everyone else go first. He
seemed to Eugene to be watching for the last time his
tattered legions passing in review: the man with the
handkerchief pressed to his skull, the woman with the
hurt knee, the man with the arm held close, even
Gregory, onto whose face fresh blood had begun to
trickle. Then himself and Mr. Economu. The priest's
face was drawn and impassive, and it occurred to Eugene
that if his cares were to be stripped from him one by one
he would be left, underneath, with only a naked despair.

Eugene helped Mr. Economu into the front seat of

the car, next to Father Carusone. He shut the door and stepped back. The window rolled down rapidly and Mr. Economu held out his hand. Expecting a farewell hand-shake, Eugene took it in his own.

The car sped off with Mr. Economu waving back at him. Eugene, looking down at his hand, saw that the man had rescued his handkerchief from underneath the chair. He was about to drop it into the gutter, but put it into his pocket instead. Then he raised his hand to wave back.

3

David Stokes's mother clasped her cardigan together at the neck, leaving exposed the front of her dress, which showed the line and curve of her breasts. Her hand was plump, and as she plucked nervously at the top of the sweater, her fingers looked like a row of newborn sucklings stumbling over each other in a blind effort to feed.

"David, he doesn't live here. He isn't here with me at all any more. I . . . I thought everybody knew that." She backed away from him.

Eugene didn't know whether her terror was of him or for the trouble her son might be in. "Could you tell me where I can find him?"

"He's a good boy. Never any trouble to anyone." She tried to smile, as if it might distract Eugene from his purpose for being there, but the lips came too close together and she had to swallow before she could part them. She took another step away from Eugene, breathed a deep breath, and looked at him directly, waiting, ready for his next assault.

The kitchen where they stood was immaculate and polished. The gleam of the linoleum reflected back the shine of the stove, the refrigerator, and the metal cabinet against the wall. The towels on the rack near the sink were folded perfectly, and so was the dishcloth. A washed coffee cup and saucer were drying on the drainboard, but the spoon, apparently, had already been put away. The Formica-topped table in the middle of the room had as its centerpiece a small glass filled with toothpicks, as though this were the only type of bouquet appropriate to such surroundings. The glass itself was placed absolutely in the center.

Eugene couldn't help reflecting that this was exactly the kind of kitchen he'd wished for all the time he was growing up: obsessively clean, instead of cluttered and chaotic, as it had been on the farm. His grandmother enjoyed sewing, carpentry, baking, working in the garden, and knitting, and she managed, aside from cooking three hasty meals a day, to divide most of her time among her preferences, while exercising an almost total indifference to the requirements of ordinary housekeeping.

Her large round kitchen table would hold at any given time, not a simple glass of wooden toothpicks, but the pliers, the sugar bowl, the sewing basket, the cream pitcher, two or three jars of jelly, a screwdriver, the butter, some plates with half-eaten pieces of bread, the coffeepot, at least two cups not necessarily on saucers, a prayer book, a floured rolling pin, her scissors, a flashlight, a partially knitted sock complete with needles, a pan of rising bread dough, a hammer, a scattering of safety pins and nails, mittens in the winter and, for some reason, stockings in the summer, and the yolk of a cold fried egg. Once a muddy trowel stayed there for a week, until it was pushed off onto the floor to make room for rolling out some cookie dough.

A similar chaos reigned throughout most of the house. For the moment, Eugene envied David Stokes that this was the kitchen he would come home to. But the feeling made him ashamed, as though he had hurt his grandmother without meaning to. So he wouldn't see her wounded but unreproachful eyes, he looked again at Mrs. Stokes.

In the glare of the overhead fluorescent, he could see that her eyes, like her son's, were dark, but frightened and tired. Her face was not so much fat as full, with round cheeks and a small nose with tender fleshy nostrils. Her mouth, too, was small, but the lips, like the nostrils, were fleshy and full. Her brown hair was long and brought back behind her ears by a pink ribbon tied at the nape of her neck. Her ears were small but, again, too fleshy to be considered delicate. Eugene suspected that she liked them to be seen.

"I'm not accusing David of anything," he said. "I just want his help, is all. Like I said, Father Carusone at the church sent me."

This was the lie that Eugene had told to get himself into the apartment, and he was ready to go right on using it as long as it seemed helpful.

"Did Father say he stole it?"

"No, of course not. Can't you just tell me where I can find him?" Mrs. Stokes took another step backward. Eugene continued. "There's a reward," he said.

"I give him money." She drew herself up defiantly. Her eyes were pleading, begging Eugene to believe her. "You think I don't give him any money, but I do. Five dollars last Sunday, and I gave him ten dollars Tuesday. To give to Daniel's mother, because I don't want him to be any trouble."

"Who's Daniel?"

"Father didn't tell you? Another boy from the school. David stays with his family now. Why didn't Father tell you, instead of sending you here?"

"Where's Daniel live?"

"Over near the park."

"What address?"

"How should I know? Ask Father."

"What's Daniel's last name? Do you remember?"

"Ask Father." She took another step away from him.

Eugene almost followed her but didn't want to frighten her more than he had already. He could see now that she didn't shave her legs, nor was she wearing stockings. The soft black hairs seemed to give her calves the tender touch of a dark down. Guessing that she didn't shave under her arms either, Eugene realized that the sweet musky odor he had smelled when she opened the door came, not from the apartment, but from her. It wasn't that she was unclean; merely natural.

When she saw Eugene looking at her legs, she pulled the sweater closer around her neck, the fingers no longer nervous but clamped now in a hard fist at her throat.

Eugene, to make her feel safer, took a backward step himself. "I don't want to get him into any trouble. I only need his help. Please. Can't you even remember Daniel's last name?"

"I don't have anything to do with Daniel. Ask David. Ask Father. It doesn't have anything to do with me."

"Does Father Carusone know? I mean, where I can find Daniel?"

"David did not take your camera! Why would anyone say he did?"

Before Eugene could repeat that he wasn't accusing the boy, Mrs. Stokes took her hand away from her throat and let the sweater open at the neck. She dipped into her cleavage and pulled out a black cloth coin purse with a clasp like two small silver knuckles. "I don't want him to cause anyone any trouble."

She opened the purse and took out a roll of dollar bills. "You'll only scare Daniel's mother if you go over there. How much did the camera cost?" She began to fumble with the bills, as if hoping they would multiply in the confusion. There couldn't be, by Eugene's count, more than seven or eight, all singles.

When the door opened behind Eugene, Mrs. Stokes closed her hand around the money without looking up. Quickly she shuffled the bills back into the purse, her eyes keeping watch on what she was doing.

Eugene turned, hoping to see the boy.

The man was tall and lean, with a prominent adam's apple that looked like a second nose. There had been two names on the bell downstairs. This must be R. Zalensky. His hair had streaks of pure yellow and pure white, waved back and neatly trimmed. He wore gold-rimmed glasses, and the way he held his thin lips pressed primly together suggested that he considered himself quite handsome. On his green denim shirt, the words *Statmier's Hardware* were stitched in maroon script. Mrs. Stokes did not look at him as she tucked the purse back into her cleavage and pulled her sweater closed.

"Who's this?" When the man smiled, Eugene saw a row of perfect teeth the color of the blond strands in his hair.

"I'm looking for David," said Eugene.

Still smiling and without reacting at all to what Eugene had said, the man slapped him on the face.

"He's from the priest!" screamed the woman.

The man slapped Eugene again, still smiling, not disturbing the glasses on his nose or the hair on his head.

"He's from the priest, I told you!"

This proved to be no protection. With Eugene too surprised to fight back, the man simply kept slapping him, not so much to hurt him as to steer him out into the hallway. This accomplished, the man, still smiling, closed the door.

When Eugene raised his fist to pound on it, he heard another slap from inside. No sound followed. He heard the slap again, then nothing, not even a whimper. He could see the man still smiling.

4

ꙮꙮꙮ

Turning the corner onto his own block, Eugene walked down the deserted street, dimly lit, with the parked trucks adding to the shadows. He went past the iron-shuttered warehouses, the loading platforms littered with scraps of cloth and splintered crates, empty metal drums, and squashed cardboard boxes. The street looked as though it too had seen a riot, some fierce upheaval, with the hulking trucks left behind to brood over the abandoned battlefield.

The night air was chilly. Eugene put his jacket on and slung the pouch with the backup camera over his shoulder.

His selfish pleasure at the news of Johnny's death had disappeared. Perhaps it had been a temporary protection from a deeper feeling, or an emotion produced by shock. In any event, what he felt now was a simple world-weary grief. His ready desires of the night before had been tempered into longing, a longing that was safe now because it could never be satisfied. Grief, in its own way, had become a form of comfort.

Eugene felt as well a certain sense of relief. As eager as he had been to meet Johnny, there was, at the same time, a definite anxiety over what Johnny would really be like and how their relationship would actually turn out. There had been, from the beginning, the possibility of Johnny's rejecting him, angry perhaps and scornful, even violent. Or it could all have been exactly what Eugene had hoped for. But what would that have led to? Where would it have gone from there?

Now all these questions were, if not answered, at least withdrawn. The anxiety had been resolved and Eugene couldn't help feeling somewhat relieved. If he had been denied a possible gratification, he had also been spared a potential complexity, even if it took Johnny's death to do it.

Thinking of his grandmother's death, Eugene recalled that then, too, he had felt relieved, even though he loved her and would have died himself rather than see her harmed in any way. Now he wouldn't have to worry about her any more. There, too, it had been an anxiety assuaged. Is it possible, he wondered, that all deaths provide this same relief, that we secretly wish for them because, after all, they put to rest with such easy finality all those anxieties we could never resolve ourselves?

But, when the idea presented itself, Eugene decided

to let it pass. With the sting of R. Zalensky's slaps still smarting on his face, he thought he deserved a little peace, a time emptied of thought, where he could draw his losses about him like a warm quilt from home and feel nothing beyond comfort and protection.

He trudged up the four iron-plated steps leading to the outside of his building. At least Helen wouldn't be there waiting for him, requiring an account of the day's events. That much pleased him. Or did it?

He had looked at her just before he left the loft that morning. She was sleeping on her mattress on the floor of the storeroom, an old army blanket pushed down almost to her ankles. In her white flannel nightgown, her pudgy young body looked like a batch of his grandmother's bread dough expanding lazily under a floured meal sack. Her breasts, two plump loaves, sagged down on either side, like weights anchoring her to the mattress. Her right arm was crossed over her eyes and her left arm was raised straight over her head, as though she had been sending a signal in semaphore but had fallen asleep before completing the message. Typical of Helen, she formed no known letter, coming closest to a *w*, which, it occurred to Eugene, could stand for all the questioning words: who, where, when, what, why.

All Helen had needed was a place to stay for a month or so, which was fine with Eugene. She could have the storeroom. She knew there'd be no sex between them. But when he saw her begin to fall in love with him, he did nothing to discourage it. To him, Helen was a joke. Her feelings flattered him. And so, one rainy restless Sunday afternoon, about three weeks ago, as a joke, he'd made love to her.

For two days afterwards he managed to convince himself it was Helen he loathed. She was repellent. She was fat and she was sloppy. She was stupid. He was allowed to think this, however, for only those two short days. Then he realized it was himself he loathed. Since then he had struggled to get the burden of his loathing back onto her, but he never completely succeeded, and the continuing battle had exasperated and exhausted him. That's why he had been drunk three times this week.

Looking down at her that morning as she slept, Eugene had thought of waking her to say goodbye. She was leaving the loft and moving in with a new friend, a waiter at Maxwell's Plum. Eugene wanted to offer some sort of final comfort, comfort as much for himself as for her. Helen snorted in her sleep and he noticed she was breathing half through her mouth and half through her nose. The one thing he had always been able to hate about Helen was her nose.

It was such a dainty little nub, placed so delicately amid the other pale and pimpled parts of her face that it seemed a pretension. By rights, Helen should have a nose like a truck driver's, except, of course, for the hair sticking out. But no, she had managed to appropriate this tiny little tip, perfectly shaped, angled almost exquisitely against her face. With a nose like that, Helen could lay claim to a sensitive, sweet, and vulnerable nature, as though that one feature were capable of negating the general plainness of the rest of her bulky body. He resented it. The real Helen, he knew, was in that nose. He had not waked her. He had not said goodbye.

Just as he was about to put the key into the lock, Eugene saw a bum sleeping on the loading platform next to the steps. Usually he would have waked him up and asked him if he wanted to sleep in the downstairs hallway, especially if it was cold and looked like rain, as it did tonight. But he was too tired to bother.

He opened the downstairs door. The light from the inside hallway cut across the sleeping figure and Eugene saw the tan jacket with the sleeves unbuttoned at the cuffs. He saw the gray corduroy pants and the brown hair falling across the scarred cheek. It was David Stokes. He was curled up facing the huge iron warehouse door, sound asleep, his fists stuffed into his pockets.

Eugene slumped against the doorway with relief. His career, his life were back in motion. There was David Stokes, obviously come to bargain for the camera's return. Eugene squatted down over the sleeping form. "David?" The boy didn't stir. Eugene touched his shoulder, but David only curled his knees in closer. "David? Wake up." Eugene rocked the shoulder a little. "David?"

The boy jumped up, pulling his fists from his pockets, turning one lining inside out so that it dangled like a dog ear. His eyes were wide open, his whole body drawn back into a half crouch as if ready to spring if he

(5 1

were cornered or attacked. He was looking at the huge metal door of the warehouse, cocking his head in quick jerks like a nervous bird.

The movements stopped. "Is it locked?" he whispered.

"You still asleep?" Eugene had tried to speak in a normal voice, but it, too, came out a whisper.

The boy drew close to him, still staring at the door. He leaned himself into the groove between Eugene's arm and his side, an instinct toward touch that seemed not only an appeal for protection but a plea for assurance that what had to be faced would not be faced alone.

Eugene felt the boy's warmth and could smell a sugary sweetness blunted by a scent of dust, but the hair that brushed against his jaw was almost soothing. It smelled salty and clean. There was a pale pink scratch down the cheek that hadn't been there before, and the dark smudges on the chin and nose looked as though the boy had been thrown face-down in the dirt.

"You're still asleep. Wake up," Eugene said, his voice still a whisper.

The boy crouched even deeper into Eugene's side, still watching the enormous metal door. Eugene looked at it himself and felt a tremor, as though the boy's fear were contagious. For a moment it seemed that they were both waiting, together, for a revelation or a vision that would, in his grandmother's phrase, "scare the living daylights" out of them.

Eugene deliberately shivered his whole body to

shake off the tremor and shake off the boy as well. "Wake up!" he said.

Slowly David went to the door, touching it first with the tips of his fingers, then with the flattened palms of his hands. Rolling the fingers into a fist, he knocked, first lightly, then harder.

"Cut it out!" said Eugene, partly because the noise irritated him, but also because he worried that the warehouse door might, after all, open wide.

Without turning toward him, David said, no longer whispering, "I was asleep!" He laughed and jammed his fists back into his pockets. Turning to Eugene, he smiled as though proud of the accomplishment. "I was really asleep, wasn't I?"

"You were dreaming. Something about the door."

Still smiling, the boy shrugged. It no longer seemed important. But after this quick show of bravado, he was shy. He cocked his head to one side, so he wouldn't be looking directly at Eugene. "You all right? You didn't get yourself hurt or anything?" he asked.

"I'm all right," said Eugene. David nodded without saying anything further, then simply stood examining the platform with casual but unbroken interest.

Eugene wondered if it was up to him to begin negotiations, and he wondered even more how he should go about it. Dealing with thieves was, Eugene knew, a New York experience, and he was anxious not to appear ignorant of the prescribed rites. To be considered anything less than a native after five years would be painful.

Eugene knew he didn't have hayseed in his hair and never had, but he was extremely fearful that someone might make the mistake of thinking he saw it there. He was very much relieved when David himself broke the silence.

"I was just wondering," David said, still not looking at Eugene, "were you all right. One guy got hisself killed."

"I know. One of the soldiers," said Eugene. "Someone named Johnny."

"Yeah," the boy said. "You were taking his picture."

"You know him? I mean, was he a friend of yours?"

David shoved his fists deeper into his pockets. "No," he said, shaking his head sideways. "I don't know any of them."

He still wouldn't look directly at Eugene. He rearranged his lips, swallowed, and simply stood there on the platform. He seemed to be waiting with a sort of shy modesty for Eugene himself to make the first move.

Eugene gathered that it was up to him to mention the camera. "I just came from your apartment," he said, trying to sound "experienced."

David looked at him, instantly alert. "My apartment?" He pulled his fists from his pockets and slowly lowered them to his sides as though he were going to have to defend himself. "What do you mean, you been to my apartment?" There was a look of panic on his face.

"I talked to your mother," said Eugene.

"Oh. My mother's apartment." David relaxed, the crisis obviously over. *His* apartment must mean Daniel's apartment, where he was staying. *That* was the apartment he didn't want visited. Eugene saw no reason to pursue it.

"I also saw Mr. Zalensky," he said.

David merely nodded, as though that was to be expected.

"Who is he anyway, Mr. Zalensky?"

"He takes care of us," said David, ashamed of what he was admitting. But then he put his fists back into his pockets and stared sideways down at the cement floor again. "What'd you go over to there for?" he asked, trying to sound unconcerned.

"I was looking for you."

"Were you scared I got myself hurt?" He seemed to like the idea that Eugene had thought of him, even worried about him.

Eugene realized negotiations were going to be more protracted than he'd originally expected. To speed things up, he said, "No. I was looking for my camera."

The boy was more puzzled than disappointed. "Your camera?"

"I want it back."

"You got your camera right there." David pointed to the pouch.

Eugene had to admit the boy did a good job of appearing puzzled. "No, the other one," he said.

"The other one?" The boy still looked puzzled.

"That's right. The other one. Where is it?"

David blinked, slowly separated his lips, then blinked again. "You think maybe I saw someone swipe it? I didn't. I never saw anybody do anything to it. I would've stopped him." The idea seemed to please him, because he started to smile. "That's what I was hanging around for so much," he continued with growing assurance. "That's right. To make sure nothing happened. I was watching out for the camera. Why didn't you stick closer? Then nobody could've stole it."

It was clear that the boy was lying, that this was an entirely new and spontaneous explanation for his persisting presence during the parade. He couldn't even keep a broad smile from breaking out across his face, a self-congratulation for his ready inventiveness. He continued to smile as though waiting for Eugene to signal appreciation of his ingenuity.

Eugene was far from appreciative. The lie and the pleasure David took in it angered him. He was being challenged, even taunted, and he had no intention of letting the boy get away with it. Or with the camera.

"Come on," Eugene said, "you know where it is. And I'm too tired to play games."

The boy tried to laugh. "You think I . . . I . . . ?"

"I'm not going to make any trouble. I just want it back. Okay?"

"I don't have it." Still smiling, the boy hunched his shoulders up, then let them drop, as if that showed he was concealing nothing.

Eugene figured it was now *his* turn to show some ingenuity. "How'd you know where I live?" he asked. Before David could come up with an answer, he went on: "My name and address are on the camera. Isn't that how?"

"Look on the pouch too. That's where I read it. And besides, why would I come here if I was the one stole it?"

The boy was still insisting on the game and enjoying it very much, playing it, as he did, to perfection. Perhaps this was the New York way. At home, when a guilty person is rightfully accused, he confesses. To be a thief was one thing, but to be a lying thief was completely unacceptable.

The thought, however, recalled to Eugene all those times in the sixth grade when he'd stolen dimes from his grandmother's egg money to buy candy bars or Twinkies to eat in his room after school, and how, when she'd asked him once (only once!) if he'd taken a dime (*a* dime!) from the five-pound sugar sack over the sink, he had said no with a sort of disturbed innocence that pretended not to even know what the accusation meant. He also continued taking dimes right into the seventh grade, but then that year he was given his first camera for Christmas and that, for some reason, seemed to have cured him.

Angry and ashamed, Eugene grabbed David by the arm. "I want that camera back, or do I break your arm?" He was too familiar with deception to be taken in by it or to let someone else get away with it the way he had with his grandmother.

Eugene squeezed until he could feel his thumb

against the bone. David, instead of showing pain, looked directly at him. The smile was no longer there. A disappointment, deep, had come over him, as though Eugene had failed him in some profound and unexpected way. He seemed sad rather than angry, resigned rather than combative. Eugene let go. David looked at him one more moment, then turned toward the warehouse door. He stared at it, thoughtful, as if trying to locate himself, to remember where he was and why he was there. Then, without looking back at Eugene, he went down the steps and started walking toward the corner.

For a single quick moment Eugene believed the boy hadn't taken the camera after all, that he was telling the truth. But the lie had been too obvious, the self-congratulation too blatant. "That's what I was hanging around for," the boy had said. It had to be a lie. But Eugene also knew that he himself had made a terrible mistake. What made him think David had come there to admit the theft outright? Even in Iowa, they didn't insist on self-incrimination. What Eugene should have said was that the camera was stolen and would the boy please help him get it back. Instead, he had been hasty, stupid, and, worst of all, inexperienced.

"All right," he called out agreeably, as if he were surrendering to superior logic, as if the boy had really convinced him. "You didn't take it." He was ready to subscribe completely to all the rules of the game. "I . . . I shouldn't have accused you that way. I . . . I'm sorry." He was even making reparation for his mistake. Surely this should be enough. He expected David to stop, but he didn't. He kept right on walking.

Eugene went down the steps and followed, keeping about twenty paces between them, so there'd be no hint of pressure or threat. As they moved in and out of the shadows cast by the parked trucks, the boy was sometimes in the light and Eugene in the dark, sometimes the reverse. They never shared the same light or the same shadow.

Each time David emerged from the dark up ahead, Eugene hoped to see a change in attitude indicating he was willing to begin again. But the boy walked on, looking at buildings, at truck fenders, at windows, or at the corrugated warehouse awnings overhead. The exaggerated movements of his head, the whole chin lifted when a tilt would have done the job, showed he was pretending an occupation, to prove to Eugene that he had other things on his mind than the person who was following him.

Eugene was tired and hungry. He'd eaten nothing since the pancakes the night before. Still, he walked on, careful not to catch up. Before he got halfway to the corner, something disturbed him, something he didn't quite understand. Then he understood. This was the way he would follow someone when he was out searching for sex. The spatial relationship was identical, the overcasual footfalls the same, the pretended indifference to each other's presence—all this was such an exact duplicate of those other times that it generated a sexual consciousness of the boy, making Eugene aware that it had been peculiar and sweet when the half-slumbering body had leaned so easily into his own in front of the huge iron door.

Eugene stopped walking. He stood completely still, looking ahead until he was able to see David for what he was and no more: an under-age thief who had taken his camera, taunted him with the theft, and whom he was now following down the street for the sole purpose of getting his property back.

David continued from shadow to light, from light to shadow, and Eugene followed. The boy turned the corner. Here, too, there were trucks and shadows, with David appearing and disappearing as he walked.

Watching him as he crossed a patch of light, Eugene saw that the collar of his jacket was partly ripped off and flapped against his back like a noiseless scourge. Eugene thought he was too tired to keep going. He wanted to call out to the boy, ask him to wait, even beg him outright and unashamedly for a new set of negotiations. But he kept right on walking.

It seemed to Eugene now that he was being lured by the boy, back to the neighborhood, that David had been sent to lead him there, to effect his return, for a purpose Eugene couldn't even dimly guess. It was as though the procession, the theft of the camera, even Johnny's death, had been merely a prologue foreshadowing and at the same time concealing what was yet to come.

David turned another corner. Eugene followed. The

sidewalk ahead was completely empty. The boy had vanished. Eugene stopped. He listened for the sound of footsteps. He heard nothing but a car on a distant street. Walking a few steps more, he waited again, this time in a light filtering down from a warehouse window. He looked behind him, then ahead.

"All right, then. I'll get you the camera."

Eugene turned. The boy was standing about ten feet behind him, examining a scrape on his right elbow made through a rip in his jacket. Eugene had walked right past him without seeing him.

Turning the corner back onto Eugene's street, they walked quietly toward the loft. There had been a brief squabble during which David emphasized Eugene would have to write down the make and serial number of the camera to identify it and to prove it was the one he was looking for. They were on their way to do it now.

Eugene had to keep reminding himself that this was all a necessary part of the game they had to play. David could never admit to having taken the camera. The search, the actual finding, had to appear as complicated as possible. David had even said, "You don't ask any questions, right?" And Eugene had readily agreed. Also, there was to be a reward. David suggested twenty dollars, and Eugene almost blurted out that he could get much, much more, but he kept his mouth shut. It was also agreed that the camera could not be broken or the film tampered with. When David had said, "Don't worry, everything will be okay," Eugene was tempted to ask him with full sarcasm how he could be so sure, but again he kept his mouth shut.

The arrangement was not without its advantages. After giving David the make and serial number, Eugene could follow him, unseen, to where he lived. If future dealings were necessary, he wouldn't have to go through Father Carusone or R. Zalensky.

They were almost back to the loft. Without looking at Eugene, David said, "You don't live in much of a neighborhood, do you?"

Eugene hardly expected criticism from someone he considered a slum dweller. "I like it here," was all he said.

Before opening the downstairs door, Eugene showed David the rope that would ring a bell in the loft. David wanted to pull it, but Eugene stopped him. It wasn't a toy.

The boy followed Eugene into the hallway. He stopped, looked around, and sniffed the air. "You got rats, huh?"

"No," said Eugene, starting up the shredded wooden stairs, "I do not have rats."

"No?" David seemed genuinely surprised.

"No," said Eugene, closing the subject. They reached the second landing and started up to the third floor. "One more after this," Eugene said.

"You got 'em in the basement, I bet."

Eugene decided the best way to end the speculation was to agree. "Maybe. In the basement."

"Yeah," said David. "I told you. You got rats."

Coming up to the fourth landing, Eugene saw a light under the door to the loft. He put his key into the lock.

"It's open," called a voice.

Eugene opened the door. Helen lurched up out of the rocking chair by the fireplace at the far end of the room and stood there, blinking through her steel-rimmed glasses, smiling, and nervously fingering a half-empty wineglass.

5

Helen started toward them, tripping over a pair of Eugene's dungarees lying in the middle of the floor. She stopped, walked back to the table near the fireplace, put down the wineglass, then went past Eugene and David toward a coat rack near the door.

"I'm going, I'm going."

Eugene had seen her drunk only once before, on Christmas. Almost half of the gallon of red wine he'd bought yesterday was gone. He watched her impassively. "You want some help?"

"No, no help." She took a light blue sweater from the rack and began putting it on. When she saw David she stopped, with only one arm halfway into a sleeve. David again stretched his T-shirt up over his nose like a mask. Helen peered closer, purposely squinting her eyes. David let the T-shirt fall back to his chest. Helen shrugged, then continued to fight her way through the arm of the sweater.

"The Nikon got swiped during a riot." Eugene spoke calmly. "He's going to help me get it back."

"I really was going to be gone," said Helen. "Everything's moved out, but I didn't know what to do with my keys. I couldn't lock them inside and I didn't want to leave them dangling in the door outside. And God knows I didn't want to take them with me for future use."

She walked a very straight line back toward the table and began shuffling among the coffee cups, the oatmeal bowl, the refrigerator pan, paperback books, an apple core, and a bowl with a pear, some grapes, two ball-points, and a coat button. She picked up the button, examined it closely, then placed it next to one on her sweater. It didn't match. She dropped it into her wineglass.

Eugene turned to David. "I'll write down my telephone number too. When the camera turns up and you can't get it by yourself, I mean if somebody wants the reward first, you call me."

"I know what to do." Eugene was sure he did.

Helen picked up the apple core. "Is this yours or mine?" She took a nibble. "Umm. Not bad. I'll leave you the rest." She put it in the fruit bowl and searched for the keys on top of the dresser near the high loft bed.

The dark green blanket hung down like bunting. She picked up a T-shirt on the dresser and looked underneath, then pushed some pennies around, which in turn caused a belt to fall to the floor. "Do I give *him* the keys or what?"

Ignoring Helen, Eugene spoke to David in a low voice. "Wait right here. I've got the serial number in the darkroom."

"You got a darkroom?"

Starting toward the door, Eugene repeated, "Wait right here."

"Can I see it?"

"Just wait."

"Maybe they're in the kitchen," said Helen. "The keys." She walked to the middle of the room and stopped, looking down at the dungarees crumpled on the floor. "I'm sorry I didn't clean up," she called to Eugene, kicking the dungarees aside. She continued toward the kitchen but stopped again at the door. "As a matter of fact, I did clean up. I had the bed made and got all your shit picked up in here. But when I started to do last night's dishes and the ones from this morning, I changed my mind. I put everything back where it was. I'm not sure the pennies are in the right arrangement on the dresser, but the position of the apple core is fairly accurate. I had to pick it back out of the garbage. Maybe the bed isn't mussed the way it should be, but I tried. I liked punching the pillows best. Only one thing I couldn't get back the way it was. The dust. I tried to make up for it by strewing some ashes from the fireplace. The only thing I did in the darkroom was expose myself. But since I was using it as a bathroom, which it really is, I should think that's allowed."

She turned to David. "You know, I think he sometimes goes in there and enlarges himself?" She called to Eugene. "Are you in there enlarging yourself?"

Eugene had met Helen in the graveyard of St. Paul's Chapel on lower Broadway after a performance of the *Messiah* just before Christmas. She had come with Wyatt, a painter who worked part-time, the same as Eugene, for Prime Movers. Helen and Wyatt lived in Wyatt's studio just below Canal Street, and Eugene was invited for Christmas dinner. Helen made a stew and Eugene brought a poinsettia plant instead of the expected wine, which meant they had to keep drinking rum even with the stew.

When Wyatt threw Helen out late in January, she moved in with Eugene, presumably for a month, until she could find some new friend. For the first two weeks they talked and laughed a lot because they made each other nervous. Helen worked in a spice shop in the Village and brought home strange roots that she'd plant, with the promise they would flower in the spring. She also brought home spices, but she never used them in her cooking, which was limited to spaghetti, stew, several kinds of chicken, and a meatloaf of her own invention whose main distinction was that it fell apart somewhere between the pan and the plate.

Coriander was Eugene's favorite spice because of the sound.

When Eugene didn't come home at night, Helen was at first amused, then indifferent. Sometime in February, however, indifference changed to tolerance, and by the Ides of March, tolerance had become hurt.

She continued to bring home spices from the shop, and by the time she admitted to Eugene that she was in love with him, he had the most impressive spice collection south of the Village.

Then came the restless rainy Sunday. One week later, over a blackened broiled chicken, Helen announced she'd found a place to live and was leaving the loft.

Eugene came out of the darkroom, walked past Helen, and handed a piece of paper to David. "Can you read it all right?"

"Can't I see the darkroom?"

"Sorry," said Helen, returning to the table and shifting the clutter around again. "Nobody gets to go into the darkroom unless he or she has to go. Even then, he almost tags along to make sure you don't touch anything except the toilet paper." She picked up her wineglass and drank the rest, spitting back the button. "I meant to finish all your wine, but I don't think I made it. Sorry."

Eugene saw that David was staring at Helen. "She's not always like this." He took him by the shoulder and started him toward the door.

"Oh yes she is," said Helen, nibbling again on the

apple core. "Only it doesn't always show. You see, kid, or whatever your name is—"

"David."

"David. I'm Helen. You see, kid, Helen has several disguises, all of them menial. Sometimes she's the maid, dusting, doing dishes, shopping, laundry, the usual shit. Then sometimes she's best friend, cozy, encouraging, inflating, lying, you know. The usual shit."

Eugene began to open the door for David. The boy, walking backward, continued to watch Helen.

"Then sometimes," she said, "she's rejected lover, self-pitying, plotting, loathing, unappetizing. You know. The usual shit."

"Does she live here?" asked David, still staring at her.

"No," answered Helen. "She used to. But this very afternoon she moved all her effects and finery out, including a picture of herself taken on a winter Saturday by that asshole standing there."

Eugene pushed David closer to the door.

"Wait," said Helen. "I haven't found him his set of keys."

"Okay," said Eugene, "cut it out."

"I know I left them some place. Ah. Of course." She shook a copy of *The Soho Weekly News*, and the keys plopped noiselessly onto a towel bunched up near the fruit bowl. Helen picked up the keys and started toward David. She tripped again over the dungarees.

Jangling the keys, she said to David, "Remember now, he likes grapefruit juice instead of orange, and coffee strong. Don't talk to him until after he's been to the bathroom. He's a little sloppy, but you get used to it."

David, staring at her, moved his hand as though to accept the keys. Eugene grabbed them away.

"Oh. Aren't they for him?" Helen opened her mouth wide in mock surprise. "I hope I didn't say or do anything *untoward*." She smiled at David. "My mistake. Mmm. What a nice plump boy."

"Plump?" David, being skinny, repeated the word as though he'd never heard it before.

Helen, still smiling, reached out and pinched his cheek. David tried to pull back, but she hung on and began shaking the boy's head back and forth. He screwed up his face in pain.

With the downstroke of his hand, Eugene broke the hold. Helen looked at Eugene, puzzled, and rubbed her arm just below the elbow, where the hand had struck. She looked again at David, who backed away. Slowly she raised her hand as though to touch his cheek, only this time gently, but Eugene shoved the boy out into the hall. "Phone me as soon as you find out anything," he told him and quickly closed the door.

Helen stood still, her sweater dangling down her back. Eugene leaned against the door as though to prevent her from following David or to stop David from coming back in. They heard the boy's footsteps going down the stairs, slowly at first, then faster.

"Oh, well. There he goes." Helen sighed and

turned back to the room. "I wanted to finish the grapes and eat the pear, but I got too full. I did manage to use all the firewood, though. You'll have to collect some more outside. Too bad. I do believe it's going to rain. But it's supposed to rain on Easter. Did you know that?"

"Are you sure you got all your stuff out?" Eugene's voice was very even.

"Maybe I'll eat the pear before I go." She fumbled for the second sleeve of the sweater.

"You want the pear, take it with you."

"No, I think I'd rather eat it here."

"Put your sweater on. I want to follow him. I'll find you a cab on the way."

"Go follow him. I'm not taking a cab anyway."

He went to her and held up the other arm of the sweater so she could finish putting it on. "Let's go."

She moved away from him. "I don't need any help."

"Need it or not, hurry up!"

"Are you being rude to me?" She tangled with the sweater and got her fist part way into the sleeve.

"I've got to follow that kid, so will you hurry up and get the goddam thing on?"

"Go on. Follow him, I told you. What'd you let him get away for, in the first place? Although you must understand I'm a little surprised. Isn't he a bit young?"

"Stop talking garbage and get going."

"Go run after him. What do I care? I care a lot. But who cares I care? I do. But who am I? Good question. Lousy answer."

"He's got my camera. So come on, will you?"

"You go. I'll stay here and eat the rest of the grapes."

"You're coming with me."

Eugene grabbed her by the sleeved arm and half dragged her from the room. Without letting go of her, he slammed the door behind him and locked it.

"I didn't finish eating the grapes!" She sounded terrified, as though she'd failed the one task that could have been her salvation. She reached for the door knob. Eugene pulled her away and started dragging her after him down the stairs. Her fist was caught inside the other sleeve, and her crooked arm waved back and forth like a broken, featherless wing.

"If he got away—"

"I hope he's in Butte, Montana, by now." She clumped unsteadily after him as he tugged her from one landing to the next.

Outside, Eugene looked up and down the block. "Come on, he's gone around the corner."

"Let me put my sweater on. It's cold."

"You can put it on in the taxi."

"I'm not taking a taxi. I'm taking the subway."

"You're taking the first taxi we see. And stop making so much noise. I don't want him to know I'm following."

Helen started to sing. "And He shall reign for ever and ever! Hallelujah! Hallelujah!"

Eugene let go of her arm and looked at her. "Okay. Find your own fucking taxi!" They had never talked to each other this way before, not she to him or he to her, but Eugene had no time to be sorry or shocked or ashamed. He began to walk ahead.

"I'm not taking a taxi," she called after him. "I'm taking the subway so I can get myself raped."

Eugene ran to the corner and looked in one direction and then the other. He moved a few steps uptown, the way he'd followed David before, but he saw no one. There hadn't been time for the boy to get to the next turning. Eugene looked downtown, then in all four directions, but saw only a man carrying an umbrella two blocks south. He stepped out to the middle of the street and looked again, north and south, east and west. Then, at the center of the intersection, he stood still, listening more than looking. A blue Pinto heading downtown forced him back to the curb.

Helen was holding on to the pole of a No Parking sign, bending over into the gutter and throwing up. Eugene started back toward her. "Okay, he got away. You can quit now."

Helen retched again, but nothing came up. Her long hair was hanging down, shielding her face. A long streak of saliva stretched out beneath it. It snapped, slowly bounced up twice like a lazy rubber band, then snapped again and disappeared. Without straightening up, she let go of the No Parking pole and reached out an arm toward Eugene, opening and closing her hand as though trying to clutch the air. "Handkerchief," she said.

Eugene reached into his back pocket and pulled

out his handkerchief. Just as he was about to hand it to her, he remembered he'd used it to dry Mr. Economu's toes. He considered giving it to her anyway, but shoved it back into his pocket. Touching her shoulder, he helped straighten her up. Saliva and what looked like a chunk of apple hung from her lower lip, dripping down onto her chin. She was breathing heavily. Her eyes opened and closed at intervals, as though uncertain they could see. Her cheeks were wet. Eugene took the cuff of his jacket sleeve in his fist to hold it taut. He wiped her mouth and chin.

"Not with your sleeve," she said.

"Hold still."

She pushed her hair back behind her ears and let him finish cleaning her face. He wiped the wet cheeks with the heel of his hand.

"Better?"

"Not really." She closed her eyes, took in a deep breath, then opened them. "Help me with my sweater."

"You've got it twisted in back. Here. Take it all the way off."

She had trouble freeing her fist from the sleeve.

"You want to go back upstairs?" he said.

She shivered as he helped her back into the sweater.

"Maybe you better stay here tonight after all," he said.

Helen shook her head no. "Allan's waiting."

Eugene looked at her but didn't say anything. Then he took her by the elbow, only this time more gently. "Can you walk? We'll never get a cab here."

"I don't want a cab. I'm taking the subway."

"That was before you threw up," he said, as though vomiting were a way to wisdom.

"If I throw up on the subway, I won't be the first."

They started to walk. "You need some money?" He still had a dollar left in his pocket.

"No," she said. "I've got enough. Your laundry and cleaning I was going to get? Well, I didn't. I kept the money." She tried to walk faster to keep up with him. She was shivering, her arms folded to keep the sweater closed. They reached the corner and turned uptown toward the subway stop. Without looking at him, Helen said, "You mad at me?"

"Keep walking."

After half a block in silence, Helen, still not looking at him, said, "You could at least say thanks. I mean, for all the lousy things I did today. Now you don't have to feel like such a shit. Which you are anyway. But now I am too. So what difference does it make?"

Eugene picked up the pace as though hoping it would give her less breath for talking. She fell a little behind. "Am I?" she said. "Am I really a shit at last?"

"Just keep walking."

"Answer me. Am I?"

Eugene stopped. "What do I care what you are or what you aren't! I've got a camera stolen with film inside and I'm with the kid who stole it and I want to follow him so I can get it back. And then you come along and fuck up the whole thing! You think I've got nothing better to think about than what you are or what you aren't? All I want is to get you into a taxicab or a subway so you're gone. All I want is to get rid of you. You and everybody else. So I can be alone for a change. Now shut up and walk."

He started again toward the subway, but Helen stayed where she was. Eugene went back to her. "All right. Stay here!" He turned to go home. Helen didn't move. When he got back to the corner, he turned and looked at her. She was slumped against the wall of a building, half in shadow, her arms fallen to her sides. Her head was bowed.

Leaving her there, Eugene turned the corner toward his building and continued the walk home. When he reached the No Parking sign where Helen had thrown up, he stopped. With his open palm he banged the pole, so that it quivered and hummed. Pain numbed his arm.

He went back to the corner. Helen hadn't moved. He went to her. When he reached out to take her arm, she cringed, but after he'd touched it, she straightened up and let him lead her down the street. He walked more slowly than before.

No cabs went by, and when they reached the steps leading down to the subway, they stopped. Helen withdrew her arm, pulling it up against herself slowly, as if afraid that some sudden movement would endanger it. She reached the arm across her chest and rubbed her shoulder as if to soothe a bruise. Then she took hold of the top of the sweater, using it as something to grab onto, so her arm wouldn't dangle limply at her side.

Eugene stepped back and stood there waiting and ready for what he knew she was going to say. It was, he acknowledged to himself, her turn. The muscles of his face relaxed. He would take the blows stoically.

Helen looked down the subway stairs. They led to a landing where the steps turned left. The white tiles of the walls had been scrubbed and the stairs recently hosed. There was still the smell of water, almost of a fresh rain. Without a word, Helen started down the steps. She examined her foot each time she was about to set it on the step ahead of her. When she reached the landing, she let go of the sweater and took hold of the railing. Without looking back, without saying a word, she turned and continued down the steps, still examining closely whichever foot was leading the way.

Eugene waited until her shadow on the opposite wall had disappeared, then went out to the middle of the intersection, wishing a truck would come and run him down.

6

Eugene stood on the pedestrian overpass above the highway separating the East Side neighborhood from the park that ran along the river. It was still dark and it was cold. A car drove underneath, the glare of its headlights forcing him to squint his eyes. He hadn't intended to come to Mass, but after not sleeping most of the night, he thought he might just as well. Resigned to a continuing struggle, he'd ask the priest to help him get the camera back.

The night itself had passed in solitary and fruitless vigil. After leaving Helen at the subway, he had walked home in the rain, collecting empty crates and some staves from a broken barrel. He stomped and sawed the wood so it would fit into the fireplace, then cleaned up around the loft, even washing the dishes and making the bed, feeling it was some form of reparation he owed to Helen.

When David did not come by nine o'clock, Eugene ate a can of roast-beef hash and the pear. When he hadn't come by ten o'clock, he developed the film from the backup camera and made a contact print. Little he saw in the pictures interested him. It was all a tangle of faces, arms, and legs. Perhaps in the context of the pictures on the stolen film, they would be climactic, but alone they offered nothing but parodies of human expression: twisted mouths, bulging eyes, puffed cheeks, waving arms, all without motive or purpose. There were no pictures of Johnny. In the background of one, however, he did spot Mr. Economu kneeling in the vacant lot, his rosary dangling from his fingers. In another, he thought he saw the man who'd been carrying the cross punching someone, but he wasn't sure. To his surprise, Raimundo turned up four times, the pictures divided equally between defense and attack.

He also saw what could be David, staring right at the camera. Eugene looked closer, wondering if an enlargement might possibly show the Nikon already in his hand, but after examining the print through the magnifier, he realized the boy was just standing there, looking at him with easy interest, waiting, probably, for a chance to snatch the camera.

When David had not come by eleven, Eugene built a fire in the fireplace and ate the grapes, spitting the seeds into the flames, listening to the sizzle.

At one o'clock, he tried to make some prints, but

that made him even more restless than he already was. Sitting in front of the fire, he drank from the gallon of wine Helen had failed to finish, but gave up after less than a full glass. At two o'clock he jangled the bell inside the window, hoping the sound might provoke a legitimate ring, the way one bucket of water can sometimes prime a pump. The bell sounded lonely and hollow in the night.

Staring into the fire, he thought of Helen and almost wished she were there, asleep on the mattress in the storeroom, snoring as she sometimes did. He remembered the way she had looked at her foot as she followed it down the subway stairs. He saw again the last straggle of her hair as she turned at the landing. Had she waited for him like this on nights he didn't come home?

He got some music on the radio and turned it up as loud as it would go. He put more wood on the fire. At three o'clock he fried the last egg in the refrigerator and ate it, saying out loud to himself, "Oh, is that good, is that ever good," as though he were encouraging a child to eat its breakfast. He had become his own grandmother, except she had never talked so stupidly. He remembered, however, a picture he had taken of her when he was a junior in high school. She was sitting on the farmhouse porch, on the rocker, holding her fly swatter as though it were a scepter. She didn't seem to know that the hem of her dress was coming down, with loose wisps of thread hanging along a frayed edge, or that her stockings were wrinkled and sagging, or that she was going to die within a month. Eugene ate the rest of the egg in silence.

At four o'clock he admitted the boy would not come. He turned off the music and stopped putting wood on the fire. He began listening very carefully for any sound at all. The rain had stopped. A car passed a block away, squishing the wet pavement. He heard a window close far off, and the floor in the storeroom creaked twice. The fire sputtered as though spitting back the seeds it had been fed earlier. He wished he had been kinder to the boy, or that he had offered him a larger amount of money. His anger started up again, and if David had appeared at that moment, camera in hand, he would have been beaten to within an inch of his life.

But what if he had been mugged on the way over and the camera taken from him as he fought to save it? There were two assailants. Eugene heard them running as David held his bleeding head in his hands.

Eugene started toward the coat rack to put on his jacket, to go look for him, to help him, then realized he must have dozed sitting in the chair. He sat down again, trying to think no thoughts at all, to make no movement; the boy would then be forced to come, simply to fill the vacuum. The fire was ashes and the residue of the egg had hardened on the plate next to him. A car drove by on the street below, then a truck. It was almost dawn. He had waited all night and the boy hadn't come.

On the overpass, Eugene looked to his right at the long stretch of Tenth Street. He saw not one living thing, no wanderer, no stray. Even the garbage cans and the trash piled against the buildings down past the red-brick housing project seemed to sag from all that silence.

He looked to his left, into the park, and at the river beyond. The sky above the low buildings on the far side of the water was beginning to lighten, showing leaden clouds huddled sullenly along the eastern horizon.

Another car sped under him, its headlights less a glare than those of the car before. He looked down into the park, among the trees. Their branches were still bare, except for a few swollen buds on the sycamores. He looked for Father Carusone and the people who might have come to the Mass, but saw no one.

He had walked over slowly, hoping he'd get there just as Mass was ending. Perhaps he'd walked *too* slowly and everyone had already gone home. He turned and started back across the overpass. He might as well stumble back to the loft and try to get some sleep.

Before he started down the ramp, however, he heard singing in the distance. A car passing underneath cut it off, but it returned, quiet and persistent. He went back toward the park and listened. The singing had stopped, but he saw a small band of people standing in a ragged circle just off a path that ran along the embankment of the river.

The light had grown but had no brightness. It seemed merely to inflict its own drab gray on everything it touched, like an inept Midas. The people were almost indistinguishable from the landscape around them. If it hadn't been for the hymn, he would never have noticed they were there.

Eugene went down the ramp into the park. Mass was still going on. He could hear the murmur of the priest's voice and see some of the people gathered around a smoking metal drum: a woman in a dark blue coat, a tall man with blond hair combed straight back from his forehead, the woman in the full-length fur coat, a short fat man with a beard who looked like an inflated version of a Snow White dwarf. There were some younger people, teenage boys and girls, and the man who yesterday had been carrying the cross. Also a girl with glasses and with a huge scarf covering her head, who looked like a disagreeable peasant.

A gust of wind sucked a cloud of sooty smoke up out of the metal barrel like a small tornado. The circle widened, there were coughs, and everyone shooed ashes from in front of his face as though they were mosquitoes. Then they laughed and began brushing soot from each other's clothes. Eugene went nearer.

Various diagnoses and remedies were being offered for the ailing fire: they hadn't used enough newspaper, the wood was wet from the rain, they should have brought kerosene, some of the boards should be broken up so there'd be more kindling. Someone volunteered to siphon gasoline from a car on Tenth Street.

There was one mumbled suggestion that made sense. No one had thought to bang holes along the bottom rim of the barrel. There was no updraft. Without it, the fire wouldn't catch. It was useless in such heavy weather to keep trying. Everyone turned to Eugene, and he realized that, in his weariness, it was he who had spoken so sensibly.

"Then we should just let it die out?" said Father Carusone.

"Maybe, before it chokes us," said the woman in the blue coat.

"But a fire would be so beautiful. And, besides, I'm cold." It was the girl with the scarf who spoke, not disagreeable at all. "Can't we keep trying?"

"Why not make a bonfire?" said Eugene. "Does it have to be in the drum?"

"Yes. A bonfire," someone whispered as though giving assent to a revelation. Eugene looked to see who had agreed with such solemnity, but as he turned, the person who had spoken brushed past him, went to the drum, and began snatching out the charred pieces of smoldering wood. "You," he said to Eugene, "you help me." It was a young man with long black hair that curled up at his ears. A gauze bandage covered his right eye and his left hand was in a cast. It was Raimundo, Johnny's mournful friend, the soldier who had started all the trouble. There he stood, battle scars and all. Turning to the priest, Raimundo said, "This man, we should listen to him." He spoke so dolefully, however, that Eugene at first reasoned he was subdued because of the death of his comrade, but then he remembered how melancholy Raimundo had been in the restaurant when Johnny, all dazzle and enthusiasm, was persuading him to be in the procession. It was, perhaps, his nature to mourn.

The man with the straight blond hair started toward the barrel. "Okay, let's do it."

Raimundo held up his good hand to stop him from coming one step closer. He and Eugene would do it, alone. He took hold of the top of the barrel and started tilting it.

Eugene touched his arm. "Don't tip it. There are ashes at the bottom and they'll go flying all over the place."

"No, don't tip it," Raimundo repeated. "We'll take it over by the trees, but we won't dump it. We'll pick out the wood and bring it back here and get another fire going. Am I right?"

Guiding the drum with his hand, Eugene rolled it away. Raimundo walked alongside, touching it from time to time to show that he was helping. After it had been rolled far enough from the group, Eugene set it upright, and Raimundo, with his good hand, began snatching from it sticks and unburned or partially burned wood. "Hot, hot," he said, but wanly, as if it were a pitiful fact about which he felt a wistful sympathy.

The bonfire was built and Eugene, down on his knees, bent his head sideways to blow at its base. Raimundo squatted down next to him so that he, too, could blow on the fire. When it flared, he gazed into it a long moment as though he could see there some sad remembrance, then he got up. Eugene stood next to him. He was feeling less tired.

"I'll go ahead and finish my few words," Father Carusone said. He put his hands into the pockets of the heavy red-and-black-checked lumberjack shirt he was wearing over his cassock and surplice. The fire began to blaze and everyone happily stepped back a little to avoid the heat.

"I just want to add a few things to what I said already, and then we can go ahead with Mass before it starts to rain." The priest was speaking in conversational tones, looking from face to face in the circle around the fire. "Johnny," said the priest, "is dead. He was one of the meanest men I ever met."

Eugene jerked his head involuntarily. He wasn't sure he'd heard correctly. The priest went on.

"Johnny's only reason for doing anything was to try to spoil it for everyone else." Here Father Carusone glanced at Raimundo, who had started, with great concentration, to pull threads from the lining of his cast, rolling them into little balls and tossing them into the fire.

"I'm not saying Johnny started it yesterday, but like most of us, he certainly helped keep it going."

Raimundo, looking especially close at a thread ball, said quietly, "Somebody pushed me."

"I know somebody pushed you. And you pushed him back. And then he pushed somebody else. And then . . ." He stopped, then started again. "But that isn't what I'm talking about."

Raimundo threw a ball of thread into the fire and searched for the beginning of a new one.

The priest went on. "Johnny wasn't the only one to make trouble. But he is the only one who's dead. And I'm sure if a vote had been taken about who should be dead when it was all over yesterday, Johnny would have won with no difficulty at all. He would have had my vote, hands down. He would have had his mother's vote, and his sister's. He would have had the vote of anyone who knew him."

Eugene looked at Raimundo, appealing to him to correct this slander against his friend. As if sensing Eugene's need, Raimundo looked up and slowly nodded his head yes. Everything the priest was saying was true.

"Johnny died on Saturday," said Father Carusone, "and today is Sunday, Easter Sunday, the day we celebrate the Resurrection of Our Lord, Jesus Christ." Eugene bowed his head in reflex reverence at hearing the name. Raimundo was staring at the thread ball in his fingers, rolling it very slowly.

"But the real resurrection we must celebrate today if Easter is to mean anything at all," said Father Carusone, "is the resurrection of Johnny. When he died, he had no real friends, he was hated and despised." Again, Eugene looked at Raimundo. Again Raimundo nodded yes.

"His death," Father Carusone said, "was the same as the death of Christ, and the fact that Johnny wallowed in his abandonment and rejoiced in our hatred doesn't really make any difference. Crucifixion isn't really death on a cross. It doesn't even have to be death. Crucifixion is abandonment, abandonment by your brothers and your sisters. And we are Johnny's brothers and Johnny's sisters. 'My God, my God, why have you forsaken me?' That was the exact moment of crucifixion."

Raimundo saw Eugene watching him roll the thread. He smiled a little, flipped the ball into the fire, and searched for another thread.

"Today," said Father Carusone, "is Easter. Today is the day of reconciliation, the day of forgiveness. Unless we feel in our hearts that we have exchanged forgiveness with Johnny, that we have forgiven him and that he has forgiven us, we are not celebrating Easter for what it really is. We are trapped in a long succession of Good Fridays where we crucify and we are crucified, again and again and again. But when we forgive each other, and when we accept each other's forgiveness, we share in each other's resurrection."

He paused, looked into the fire a moment, then said, "When we wish each other a Happy Easter, we should remember that it's still only a wish, not a reality. It will be a reality on the day when we can say it with Johnny, who is our brother and who lived and died despised."

Eugene stood there transfixed by the little rolled balls of thread. So industrious had Raimundo been during the priest's words that the edge of his cast was completely frayed.

A tug passed on the river, blasting its horn three times, and Eugene noticed a small slit in the clouds just above the horizon. The tip of the sun could be seen passing through the opening into the clouds above, as though the tug, like the crowing cock, had summoned the dawn, the new day.

Father Carusone began a hymn which some sang in English and some in Spanish. Eugene knew it from his boyhood, "Alleluia, Alleluia, let the holy anthem rise," but he didn't think he should sing along. He was, he had to remember, no longer a Catholic. But the singing sounded so feeble. Surrounded by the trees, with the river flowing east of them and the solid wall of buildings rising beyond the highway to the west, robbed of the sight of the sun and waiting for the rain to fall, these people sang in hesitant voices their hymn of praise. It seemed to Eugene that they were all men and women of great courage and beauty. He was about to sing along, but Raimundo leaned toward him and said, "These people, they don't know how to sing." Eugene looked at him, smiled weakly, and decided not to join in after all.

Later, while they were reciting the Lord's Prayer, Eugene found himself staring downriver through the trees. He realized he had been watching someone, an indistinct shape, in the distance. It seemed to be watching him. Then it vanished, disappearing among the trees. Eugene reached out his foot and kicked a piece of wood so that the fire flared a little.

Father Carusone was saying something about peace and Eugene found himself being embraced by the girl with the glasses. It was time to exchange the sign of peace. Everyone was embracing everyone else. "Peace!" *"Felices Pascuas!" "La paz de Cristo!"* "Happy Easter!" The circle had broken completely and all inhibition was gone. The priest put his arm around Eugene's shoulders and firmly clasped his hand. Smiling, nodding his head cheerfully, he said, "Peace! And a Happy Easter!"

"Yes. Happy Easter, Father." Eugene felt rather alone, being embraced by all these generous strangers.

People were returning to their places in the circle around the fire, but Raimundo was still embracing people, however solemnly, shaking hands, clumping people on the back with his cast. When he came to his place next to Eugene, he looked at him, then threw his arms around him. "My friend who built the fire. Peace." The cast fell heavily across Eugene's back. Raimundo thumped it a few times as though he were knocking on a massive oak door. The young man's cheek was smooth and smelled of scented soap; his hair, like warm sweet oil.

Just as Eugene was about to speak his Easter wish, he saw, across Raimundo's shoulder, the figure again, only farther away, passing between two trees, moving away from the river. "Peace," he said to Raimundo more quietly than he had intended.

During Communion, Eugene kept watching the trees, waiting for the figure to appear again. A loaf of consecrated bread and a paper cup of consecrated wine were being passed from hand to hand. Each would break off a piece of bread and sip from the cup. When Raimundo handed him the loaf, Eugene hesitated. He watched Raimundo chew the bread and was tempted to break off a piece, not out of yearning for the Sacrament, or even to pretend to those around him that he was in a worthy state, but to establish a bond between himself and his companion.

It was whole-wheat bread and solid, with a light dusting of browned flour on the top crust. Several chunks had already been pulled away, releasing to Eugene's nostrils a faint breath from his grandmother's morning kitchen. "He's as good as bread," his grandmother's highest words of praise for any man, now came to Eugene's mind and he understood for the first time, without the need of mystery, that Christ and the bread he held in his hands were one. "He's as good as bread," he thought, looking at the loaf, feeling that the nature of his Redeemer had finally been revealed.

He handed the loaf to the woman in the blue coat. When the cup of wine came around, Raimundo, having seen Eugene refuse the bread, passed it directly on to her.

During the time for meditation, Raimundo began again to pull the threads from his cast. Eugene, looking downriver, saw the figure again in the mist and the early-morning dark, no longer hiding. It was standing there, looking, not toward them, but at the river.

Another hymn was sung in Spanish and in English

to end the Mass. The sun, completely invisible, had risen and, even beneath the low gray clouds, it was light, it was day. The fire Eugene and Raimundo had built began to burn lower, as if aware it was no longer needed. Eugene tried to hum the melody of the hymn but kept losing it. He turned to look at Raimundo, but his friend had moved away and was talking in Spanish to a soft-skinned round-cheeked girl who kept singing but was obviously attentive to what he was saying. Without moving her head, she would glance at him sideways, which encouraged him to speak that much more. Finally she looked directly at Raimundo, said something between song phrases that made him smile a bit. She then looked into the fire and continued the hymn. Raimundo now joined in, a little off-key, but loudly.

The hymn ended and the drizzle began. The flames had done their work, the wood was now a fierce orange ash, pulsing in its own heat, the throbbing heart of itself. Eugene kicked some dirt onto the embers. They flared and sputtered in protest, sending sparks into the air. He kicked once more. Now the fire neither flared nor hissed but accepted the wet clods without complaint, as though they were instruments of healing, cool and quieting. The rain would do the rest.

Eugene went to Father Carusone to mention David, but before he could say anything, Raimundo came up to him with the girl. "The fire, it was beautiful," said the girl.

"Thank you," said Eugene.

"This here, this is Reina. I am Raimundo."

"Eugene," said Eugene. They all shook hands, a rather strange formality after all the embracing and back-slapping they'd exchanged during Mass.

"Are you new here in the neighborhood?" asked Raimundo.

"I'm not really from around here. I came to talk to Father about my camera."

"That's right," said Raimundo. "You were the one took pictures of us yesterday."

"But it got stolen during the . . ." Eugene almost said "riot" but tried to think of something that wouldn't sound accusatory.

"The procession?" asked Raimundo easily, simply.

"Yeah. The procession."

"Is there a reward?" asked Reina.

Father Carusone came up to them before Eugene could answer. "Mr. Economu's foot wasn't broken after all. He thinks the washing cured it. He's going to say a rosary for you, the Glorious Mysteries."

"Tell him thanks."

"Did you know, Father," said Raimundo, "someone, they stole his camera at the procession."

"Is there a reward?" repeated Reina.

"I'd give almost anything," said Eugene, mostly to impress them with the value he placed on the camera.

"I'll help you find it," said Raimundo with such confidence that it sounded as though it had already been found. "So will Reina help too."

The woman in the fur came to Father Carusone and drew him away, toward the dying fire, saying a very long and very cheerful goodbye.

Turning to Raimundo, Eugene said, "If I get the camera back, I've got some pictures of you."

Raimundo's face furrowed as though he wasn't sure what was being said or implied. Were they being offered or what? Eugene, however, knew precisely what was happening. With no trouble at all, without its even being a conscious decision, a complete transfer of his plan for Johnny had been made. So easily had it happened that Eugene couldn't feel the least shred of shame over the substitution. It didn't even disturb him that Johnny turned out not to be what he had imagined him to be. It would seem that Eugene's scheme was a constant, and if Johnny was not available, Raimundo would do quite nicely.

Eugene thought he should at least pause and accuse himself of being shallow and faithless and selfish, but there wasn't that much time. He must act now.

"I have," he said to Raimundo, "a few of you from another camera that aren't bad."

"Of me? In my uniform?"

"A couple."

"Can I have one? So that I can give it to Reina?"

"If you think there's one good enough."

"Oooh . . . there is, there is."

"You'll have to come over, then, and take a look," said Eugene, trying to sound offhand.

"The pictures, Reina won't care what they look like. All she wants is me when I was a soldier. She made the costume, except for the armor on my chest." Reina smiled and put her head against his arm.

"You looked very good," said Eugene.

"I know," Raimundo said sadly. Then, brightening a little, he went on. "Tell me when I can come over to your place and see you and get the pictures."

"This afternoon?" Eugene hoped he hadn't sounded too eager.

Apparently, all was well. Raimundo nodded slowly and repeated the words: "This afternoon."

Slapping his pockets for a pencil so he could write down the address and phone number, Eugene noticed that Raimundo was looking into the distance, down the park. He looked in the same direction, just in time to see the figure disappear again behind a tree. It had grown lighter, and Eugene recognized it now. It was the boy. It was David Stokes. Raimundo continued to stare downriver.

"See something?" asked Eugene.

"No. Nobody."

Eugene let it go at that. "I don't have a pencil," he said, "but if I tell you my address, will you remember?"

"I have this memory, it's terrific," said Raimundo.

Eugene told him the address and repeated his name. He explained about the bellpull. Raimundo said the number and the name and kept repeating them until the girl did a quick impatient dance to the rhythm of the words.

"It's raining!" she said, laughing even as she complained.

Raimundo took her inside his jacket, holding her against him. "You're going to make me some breakfast. And then your mother, she's going to church. Because everyone goes to church Easter, even me. Isn't that right?" He squeezed her closer, until she squealed. Without looking back at Eugene, but repeating the name and number, he led her away.

Eugene saw that Father Carusone too had left the park and was already on the overpass with the man who had carried the cross. He hadn't had a chance to talk to him, but now it might not matter. David himself was there.

Eugene went and looked at the river, waiting for the boy to come to him. The surface of the water was gray-green, with a few floating sticks scraping against the concrete wall beneath him. A paper coffee container half filled with river water was bobbing its way toward the harbor. Out farther, a rusty tanker prowled slowly upriver, and on the far bank a church steeple shrouded in mist rose from among the low buildings that sprawled along the Brooklyn shore.

The tanker disappeared, dissolving around the bend. Eugene turned. David was standing at the guttered fire, looking down at the mound of ashes and earth. Instead of smoke, vague wisps of steam made by the drizzle falling on the charred wood curled slowly over the extinguished heap, brooded a moment, then vanished into the mist above.

The boy crouched down and, using his finger, poked at a few small pieces of half-burned wood, the way one would poke a bug to see if it was alive or not. He spoke very softly, without turning around. "I went to all the places I could, but I still didn't find it. I'll try again today."

He stood up, wiping his hands on the sides of his pants. He was wearing the same clothes as the day before. His hair, his face, his chest bared by the low loop of the stretched T-shirt, glistened with rain. The mist, which reduced everything else to shadow, had failed with him. The water shone on his flesh as he looked down, searching the heap as if he could find there what he wanted, among the ashes.

"What are you doing here?"

"I came to ask Father about the camera, and the others too, but I didn't when I saw you were here to ask them yourself. Did they know anything?"

"No," said Eugene.

Crouching down again, David stared at a stone that had been charred and smoked by the fire. Eugene followed the boy's gaze, until he too saw the stone among the ashes. He knew now that David did not have the camera, that he hadn't stolen it, that his, Eugene's, own stupidity had made him think that he had. "Okay. Thanks," he said quietly. "Don't bother to look any more. You won't find it."

"Yes, I will," said the boy, still speaking softly.

Eugene looked at him, at the shoulders hunched

forward as the boy bent over the ashes. "Go home," said Eugene. "It's raining."

The boy didn't move.

"Go to Daniel's, then."

Still the boy didn't move. Eugene was tired and wanted to sleep. The final loss of the camera, gone for good, wearied him even more than his lack of sleep, as though a long and arduous search had finally ended.

"Then come on to my place. I'll fix you something to eat," he said. As if to assure both David and himself that he was acting more out of exhaustion than out of kindness, he added, "But you can't talk. I'm too tired."

7

Eugene examined the contact print he'd made up the night before, looking now for Raimundo. With the film of the stolen camera this would have been no problem; there he had plenty, although he wasn't sure Raimundo would like to see himself as he'd been just before the riot. He might prefer a picture a little more conventional than himself weeping and appropriating another man's cross.

Eugene thought he'd found him, the long black hair, the sad pony eyes. But a closer look showed that it was merely a fist in another soldier's face. He went on looking.

Raimundo would come expecting a picture of himself and Eugene did not want to disappoint him.

At last he found him, his head tilted to one side,

his helmet gone, his hair drawn back from his face. Judging from the angle of his arm, he was about to punch one of the Daughters of Jerusalem in the stomach.

When Eugene printed up an enlargement of the head, he had reason to be pleased. There was Raimundo, indeed. Streaks of dirt provided a dynamic shadowing no artist could have devised, and the glistening sweat and tears gave the flesh and eyes a moisture only sea spray is said to bestow.

For a final print, Eugene started to block out exactly the area he wanted, but as the crayon crossed some faces still visible above Raimundo's hair, he stopped. He looked closer at the print. A face in the distance, almost a nub on the top of Raimundo's head, seemed to be looking directly at him. Eugene squinted, peered closer, then picked up the magnifier. If his memory of the scene was correct, whoever it was was standing on top of the rubbish heap where the crucifixion was supposed to have taken place.

It seemed to be David. Even this blurred sight of the boy was enough to revive the exasperation Eugene had felt that morning when he'd brought the boy home. To start with, David said he saw a rat scurry across the floor when they came into the loft. Not content to claim them for the basement, he was now placing them right in the apartment itself. Eugene's exhaustion had ruled out equal combat, so the subject was ignored.

Next, David wanted to take a shower, which meant Eugene had to dismantle half the darkroom. When asked if he couldn't shower when he got to Daniel's,

David answered that he could do it while Eugene was fixing breakfast.

Since this would relieve Eugene of his company for a few moments at least, he agreed. Then the boy had been unimpressed with the darkroom and Eugene had to explain that it looked more like itself when all the equipment was in operation. David accepted this as a possibility, but a remote one at best.

Naked, David was shy, which also annoyed Eugene. Shyness assumed an interest and Eugene resented the assumption. He'd admit to being curious, though, and couldn't help noticing that what he'd previously mistaken for scrawniness was actually a lean muscularity. David stayed turned away from him as he shed his clothes on the bathroom floor. "Use Helen's towel," Eugene had said, going out and banging the door behind him.

Eugene was scrambling eggs when David came into the kitchen, his wet hair plastered down as if he'd never come in out of the rain. He was dressed in the same damp dirty clothes as before. Eugene knew he hadn't offered him anything else, but he blamed David for not asking. Of course, nothing of Eugene's would fit, but he made the offer in the name of hospitality.

David said no thanks, protesting that everything had begun to dry out. Eugene gave in, but only up to a point. He refused to accept the deformed T-shirt at breakfast. The loop now reached halfway down to David's waist and it looked as though it had been dyed with mud. Eugene got a maroon turtleneck that had advertised itself as "one size fits all," and threw it at David, telling him to take off the T-shirt and put it on.

David didn't like the color.

If he didn't like it, he wouldn't get any scrambled eggs.

David didn't like scrambled eggs, anyway.

Then why didn't he say so when Eugene stopped on the way home to buy the eggs?

He had been told not to talk, and besides, Eugene was the one paying for them.

Well, he had to eat them, anyway, because they were all made.

He wouldn't eat them. He never did.

Then what would he eat?

A jelly doughnut. He assumed that Eugene had a jelly doughnut, because it was a Sunday. He finally ate some cinnamon toast, noting that it was the wrong kind of bread, it should have raisins. He didn't drink milk, and the coffee was criticized for being weak.

What infuriated Eugene most of all was the manner in which all these complaints and corrections were voiced. The boy's good cheer was unfailing. He had actually laughed when told there was no jelly doughnut on this, a Sunday. Also, when he saw the alleged rat run across the floor, he sounded thrilled, as though he'd seen a scarlet tanager in flight over a field of timothy. Then, on the subject of the coffee, the lack of strength was noted with delight. "This coffee, it tastes like nothing!"

When asked questions about himself, about

Daniel's, what it was like living there, David implied, but in a very general way, that all circumstances in his life were better than acceptable, that he liked it at Daniel's and he liked Daniel's mother and father and little brother, that he was good at school and his teachers liked him, even though he didn't always go. Why not? He didn't know. All he knew was that some days he didn't go. Was it because he didn't have clothes to wear? He had lots of clothes. He had a new suit for Easter, and when he put it on, he would come back and show him.

Because his weariness couldn't sustain an argument and because he certainly didn't want to be bothered by the boy later, Eugene said he believed him, that no proof was necessary.

After David had left, Eugene collapsed into a nap that was deep if not long. His exhaustion was gone when he woke up.

Looking now through the magnifier at the round blur at the top of Raimundo's head, Eugene made an additional complaint against the boy. Why hadn't he stolen the camera, the way he was supposed to? It would be there at this very moment if only David had been the thief Eugene had assumed he was. All Eugene's troubles and difficulties became, for the moment, David's fault, and there the boy stood, placid, on top of a garbage heap, indifferent to the inconvenience he was causing.

Eugene picked up the crayon again and marked the tiny square he would enlarge into the face of Raimundo, then found the corresponding spot on the negative.

Clamping it into the enlarger, he projected the face onto the paper in the easel below. When he adjusted the easel, however, it slipped, and what was projected instead was the blurred image of the boy. Eugene looked down at the cloudlike shadows, disconnected one from the other, as though the face were in the process of physically forming itself.

With extreme care, he brought the face into the sharpest focus possible, then turned off the projection light. Flicking on the enlarger itself, there in the glow of the safelight, he stared down at the pale red sheet.

He recalled the moment just before the boy had left the loft. At the door, David had said he would stay longer if he could, but promised to come again. Eugene wanted to assure him that it was all right, that he needn't come back, that nothing was wanted from him any more except his speedy departure. But Eugene had been too weak to speak. He just let the boy go. Waving cheerfully, jumping three or four steps at a time, the boy called back, "I'll see you!"

Eugene turned off the enlarger, slipped the printing sheet out of the easel, and, holding it with tongs, slid it into the developing solution, poking it down into the fluid to make sure it was completely submerged.

At the appointed time he transferred the print paper into the stop bath, then into the fixer. In the red glow of the safelight, he could see nothing but shadows of varying depth and darkness. When the necessary minute or so passed, he turned on the overhead light and looked down into the fixer.

It was David, but the enlarging process had erased all outline. It was as though the atoms that made up the face had begun to fall apart and away. A shadow of something unseen made a gash across the left cheek from the forehead to the mouth. It looked like a cavernous eye socket. The shadow, crawling downward, nibbled at the lips, which were slightly parted. It was as though Eugene, in trying to bring the boy closer, to confront him, to approach his mystery, had only induced decay. It was David decomposing who looked up at him with one rotted and staring eye.

The outside bell clanged. Eugene pulled the print from the fixer, crumpled it, and tossed it onto the porcelain top of the tub. He rinsed his hands, then reached for a towel. The crumpled print began to spring and snap open. First there seemed to be a small explosion at its center. Then a few of the edges kicked outward. The cavernous eye, now cracked and creased, looked at him sideways from inside the mangled paper. One more spasm and the eye was free. It was like the unfolding of an evil flower, erupting and retching itself into existence and lying now on the cool porcelain surface, spent but still malevolent.

The bell in the living room clanged again. Eugene threw the print into the wastebasket under the sink and finished drying his hands. The bell continued to clang. He had forgotten to tell Raimundo that one or two pulls on the rope would be enough.

To Raimundo, everything about the loft was a wonder which he took very seriously, like a grave and responsive child. The exotic and the ordinary were equally worthy of his attention. When he was shown the bell hanging just inside the window, he had, of course, to toll it a few more times, marveling at its sonority. He praised Eugene's ingenuity, that could construct such a device. The fireplace and the rocking chair were regarded as recent inventions. Testing the rocker, he was thrilled to see that it really rocked, and he asked for a live demonstration of the fireplace.

When he saw the loft bed, he vowed to build one for himself one day. He opened the closets Eugene had built underneath, pleased that they were spacious but puzzled that they weren't crammed. Where were Eugene's clothes? When told he didn't have many, Raimundo responded with the deepest sympathy, which he expressed with a sad shake of his head.

After he had hoisted himself up onto the bed and tested its strength as well as its comfort, Raimundo let his legs dangle over the side and praised the view from up there, but sadly. For him as for an aspiring poet, all things beautiful were a source for sorrow. Approval was an inspiration for elegy.

He inspected the kitchen in the back of the loft— one of Eugene's lesser improvisations—and found it extraordinary. He had never seen such a small refrigerator. Looking inside, he was dismayed to find that Eugene had so few provisions. He promised to come over himself sometime and make chili. The secret of the chili's success, Eugene was told, was that it contained no rice. Absolutely *no rice*.

Careful not to sound too involved, Eugene asked about Johnny. He was curious not only about Johnny himself but about the discrepancy between his own impression of him and the remarks made by Father Carusone at Mass.

The subject didn't seem to interest Raimundo, but he did relieve himself of a few comments along the way. Johnny was crazy. Johnny beat his mother with a shovel and spent his sister's money. Johnny wanted Raimundo to be in the procession only so he could make fun of him in the costume his woman Reina had made. Johnny would never smoke or drink. Johnny fed a cat rat poison. Johnny set fire to two buildings when they told him he couldn't play cards on the stoops. Johnny cheated at cards. Johnny said Reina smelled. Johnny was going to keep his whip and use it, he said, on a faggot who was going to come and try to talk to him after the procession. Johnny always laughed. Johnny never cried. Johnny made Julio Gomez fight his little brother on the bus when it was crowded. Johnny made fun of the girls who screamed for him. Johnny had no respect. And all this, Raimundo knew for the truth. Johnny was his best friend.

Eugene thought of asking for more details about Johnny's plan for his whip after the procession, but decided not to. He did, however, mention that the film in the stolen camera might show who the murderer was. After considering this for a moment, Raimundo seemed to have decided he didn't care. "You won't find anyone. It was too crowded."

(*1 0 7*

The thought that it could have been Raimundo passed through Eugene's mind, but he told himself Raimundo was too solemn a person; he had no anger in him. Even his chronicle of Johnny's crimes had been delivered with what sounded like a lasting sympathy for human frailty. The murderer was not, Eugene definitely decided, Raimundo.

When shown the darkroom, Raimundo was moved to silence, however momentary. Once the moment had passed, he asked all the questions: how this worked and that, how did Eugene know when to do this and when to do that. Each answer was accepted as a revelation profound and marvelous.

Eugene decided to allow Raimundo in the darkroom while he was working. A picture of himself, as yet unprinted, had been promised, and Eugene could hardly expect him to rock himself in the rocking chair until it was done.

To give the occasion a little drama, Eugene first showed Raimundo the contact print, emphasizing how difficult it had been to locate him and warning him that the enlargement of that one single frame would be less than perfect. If the stolen camera was found, Eugene said, there would be plenty of pictures, and much better. Raimundo, looking at the contact sheet, nodded his head and assured Eugene he would find the camera, that he would personally scour the neighborhood and all the hock shops until it was found. Eugene knew better than to let his hopes be revived, but he liked the idea of Raimundo's concern.

He put on the red safelight and turned out the overhead.

"No, wait! Not yet! I just saw Reina. Turn the light back on!"

Eugene obeyed. Raimundo showed him, through the magnifier, what appeared to be Reina. She was clawing the face of one of the civilians, who, when the picture was taken, was preparing to land her a right to the jaw. "Make this one."

It was not what Eugene had in mind. "That wouldn't be a very good picture of her, would it?" he said.

Raimundo looked at it again. "She's always like that. She's terrible." He smiled one of his rare smiles.

"Why," asked Eugene, "don't you wait until I've printed all the pictures sometime later this week, bigger, then you can see how she looks, and if you still want one, I'll do it."

"No, do it now. You don't have to do me. Do Reina."

Eugene had to agree. Raimundo watched patiently. A long "yeah" came out of him as the image began to emerge in the developing fluid. "Look at that woman go! She don't take no thing from no one." "Nothing" was separated into two words, so it could be given equal emphasis with "no one." He beat his cast on the tub top as if to spur her on to greater violence, even though, in the enlarged print, her adversary had been omitted, in the interest of giving her own particular charms full play. She looked as though she were performing an

(*109*

exotic rite that involved an extremely stylized movement of the hands. "She is really some thing."

So the event wouldn't be devoted exclusively to Reina, Eugene said, "I'll print yours too."

"Yeah, she'd like that."

Raimundo watched over Eugene's shoulder as his own image formed on the print sheet. His first remark was, "Reina says I need a haircut."

"No, you don't," said Eugene, for the sake of disagreeing with Reina.

"Yes, I do," said Raimundo, and the small skirmish was over. "She likes," he continued, "my eye bandage."

"Makes you look like a pirate," said Eugene.

"Yeah. That's what Reina said."

While the prints were being washed in running water, wine was poured in the living room. Raimundo sat in the rocking chair and Eugene sat on the couch.

"You know what you look like right now?" Eugene asked. "A conquistador. I've seen pictures that look just like you—the Spanish conquerors. The same black hair, long like yours."

It was true, he had seen it all, but the hair length he had deliberately mentioned as a criticism of Reina.

"Reina," said Raimundo, reminded of her, no doubt, by the mention of hair, "she doesn't want to be my woman. Today I asked her again. I buy her some flowers and I even take her mother to church for her, but she says she doesn't want to be my woman."

"Why wouldn't she want to be your woman? I mean, here you are, you're good-looking, you're considerate, and"—Eugene decided to hrow this in for a clincher—"you're intelligent."

"I know," was the mournful reward Eugene received for what he assumed was a partial perjury. Raimundo sipped his wine and made a face. "Sour!"

Eugene, who had received instruction from Helen about wine, explained it was a dry burgundy. Raimundo asked for some sugar. Eugene went on to say that Helen had said: the wine was supposed to taste like that; but Raimundo was convinced it was sour and insisted on adding sugar. Four heaping spoonfuls were put into his glass.

Satisfied with the wine in its improved state, Raimundo, with an open and heartfelt sincerity, told his good friend Eugene about the difficulty between himself and Reina. They both wanted to make love, that was obvious whenever they were together, but she was willing and he was not. Eugene, uncertain he had heard correctly, asked him to repeat that.

"She wants us to do everything. On Tuesdays, when her mother goes to the clinic. Her mother, she has veins that are bad. Her legs. She goes this Tuesday, but she told me on the way to church she lost her clinic card and she is afraid to go. They will yell at her. I told her I will go with her. Except Tuesday is when I see Reina at her house without her mother, when she is alone. That's when she always wants us to do it."

"But you don't want to?"

"I want to."

"Then why don't you?"

He shrugged. "I don't do it."

"Is it," Eugene asked, "because you think it's wrong?"

Without answering the question, Raimundo went on. "But when I tell Reina no, she starts anyway and I have to hit her. And then we fight, because she hits me back all the time. You saw on the picture. She bites. Did you know that?"

"No," said Eugene. "I never knew that."

"She bites. I'd show you one from last week, but it's under my cast. Maybe when the cast comes off, I'll show you."

"Maybe," said Eugene, "you'll have more by then."

"Maybe," said Raimundo sadly. "Except it's wrong for her to do that to me. I come when she does it. I get all sticky inside my pants."

"Oh?" was all Eugene could think to say.

"Sometimes it shows right through on my way home. It's not fair." Having said this, he jumped up from the chair. "There! See? It shows through." He pointed to a crinkly stiffened patch in the crotch of his pants leg. He tried to smooth it out. He rubbed it with his cast but to no effect. "I am going to kill her!"

"Did she bite you?"

"She must have. I was hitting her because she took off all her clothes. She has no shame. I tore her blouse."

"Well, if you were tearing her blouse, no wonder she thought it was all right to take off her clothes."

"No, I tore it after she took it off. She's going to tell her mother I tore it when it was still on, but when

I take her mother to the clinic, I'll tell her the truth and she will believe me. I mean, if she finds her clinic card."

"If Reina gives you so much trouble, why don't you forget about her?"

The very idea astonished Raimundo almost beyond expression. "But you saw her! This morning. And on the picture."

Eugene didn't exactly consider this an adequate explanation, but he knew what Raimundo meant.

He went on plaintively. "She is my woman. You didn't see when I was hitting her this morning. She had no clothes on. No clothes at all. She is so beautiful, like you have never seen. If you did, you would want her for yourself." He took a gulp of wine, spit it back into the glass, and added three more spoons of sugar.

"Don't you ever have any sex at all?" asked Eugene.

Raimundo seemed to think for a moment, then looked at Eugene and shook his head, still thoughtful. "You don't want to hear about that."

"Sure I do."

"No," said Raimundo, shaking his bowed head, looking down into his wine. "You don't want to hear about that."

"I wish," said Eugene, "there was something I could do to help you with her, with Reina." To his surprise, he meant it.

"It's all right. She is my woman," said Raimundo with such sorrow that Eugene felt ashamed. He had intended to take such easy advantage of the youth's deep and genuine distress. He decided now was not the time to intrude himself and his own needs.

The talk after that, to fill up the time until the prints were ready, was about motorcycles, because one roared past during the silence that followed Raimundo's last words about his woman. Raimundo was going to buy a Honda next summer, but he said this in his chili-without-rice tone of voice, so that Eugene asked for a free ride, safe in the knowledge that it would never happen. More wine was drunk. There would be no sugar for Eugene's coffee in the morning.

Raimundo left happy, bearing gifts for his woman, Reina. The pictures pleased him. His friend Eugene was generous and good. He would go to all the hock shops tomorrow. He would find the camera.

The grim hallway was praised for the spindles in the wooden banister. The plaster cast was clanked along them to give him music as he went.

Eugene heard the downstairs door close with a slam. Immediately he repented of his sympathy. What were Raimundo's sorrows to him, anyway? Did he really care about the difficulties with Reina? Quite the opposite, he was sure. It could all so easily be turned to his own advantage if only he had the guts to do the obvious. He had been timid, not sympathetic.

Furious with himself, he returned to the darkroom. He'd do prints of the parade, or the riot, or whatever it was called. Maybe something salable would turn up. It would be nice to get *some* kind of payment for his troubles.

The bell in the living room clanged. Raimundo had come back. Eugene's regrets, his anger had been premature.

He leaned out the window to tell Raimundo to come right up. There, down on the sidewalk, was David dressed in a suit of royal blue, complete with clean shirt and a yellow tie. He raised one of his new shoes to show Eugene.

"I'm working!" Eugene yelled before slamming down the window.

He went back to the darkroom, where, before beginning to work, he looked into the mirror over the sink. There were the ordinary brown eyes, the tawny skin. There was the generous-sized nose and well-proportioned mouth. And there was the shock of coarse hair splayed out over the forehead like a displaced cowlick.

Why had it been David Stokes instead of Raimundo who had just rung the bell? And why had he given up with Raimundo so quickly, so easily? His sympathy was stupid, sentimental. It was nonexistent. When would he be free of that neighborhood, all of them, Raimundo included? Again he had gotten nothing, nothing at all.

With his fist, Eugene smashed the mirror. One triangle of glass fell into the sink and splintered with a shrill tinkle.

8

The 35-mm. Nikon Eugene held in his hand was the right model, and for a moment he thought it might be his. But the balance was a little off and the nick on the ridge just below the viewer wasn't there. He tried to let out his disappointment by degrees for the benefit of the man he took to be Saul Lorenzo, who was proclaimed in letters of gold above the entrance to be the sole proprietor.

"That's what you're looking for. I can tell by your face. I can always tell by a face. It's an excellent instrument. One forty-five."

As Eugene turned it over in his hand, making murmuring sounds to indicate his consideration, his disappointment gave way to relief. Here his search ended; his obligation to the camera was finally, fully discharged.

He had done all that could be done, knowing it would do no good. But he'd had to try. He owed it to the camera.

He had also thought he might possibly run into Raimundo. Raimundo had, after all, said he intended to scour the hock shops. But if Raimundo was making the rounds, his path and Eugene's had failed to cross.

Eugene had started out early that morning at the police station on Fifth Street. He reported the camera as either lost or stolen, and the recording officer, when told the location of the loss or theft, paused, raised his pen from the form he was filling out, and told Eugene he'd never get the camera back.

The officer assumed Eugene didn't wish to give any further details and responded with sour surprise when Eugene insisted he take it all down. The officer resented this optimism, as though it pretended to superior knowledge, but he grudgingly took down all the facts, so wearied by the futility of his task that he could barely move the pen across the paper. Spellings had to be given at least twice, and when Eugene gave his full name, the officer looked at him as though he wanted to remember all this for the day of reckoning.

From there Eugene had begun his tour of the hock shops, and this one now was the last he intended to try. He'd covered the neighborhood beyond its broadest boundaries. He had met with civility and disdain, interest and indifference. He had also, inevitably, met the boy.

When Eugene went into the fourth of the seven

hock shops he was to visit that day, the place seemed no different from the previous three. It was the usual dark cave, a labyrinth of discards, the forgotten and the remembered, the scorned and the cherished, all consigned to an equal fate.

A man wearing the uniform of a Mister Softee ice-cream vendor was examining a case of meat cleavers. Eugene saw no one else, but as he looked around for the cameras, he heard a voice complaining from the rear of the shop. "I do too have money! How do you know I can't pay for it? I don't even know if you got anything I want and you won't even let me look. You want to see my money? Well, I'm not going to show it to you until you let me see what kind of cameras you got."

As a tired voice answered, pleading not to have his time wasted, Eugene turned the corner of a case filled with waffle irons and blenders and saw David glaring down at an old man sitting behind a table strewn with slips of paper and dusty account books. The man was fumbling among the papers as though one of them might yield an effective antidote to the boy, like a gun, for instance.

David looked up, saw Eugene, and without pausing to greet him or alter his tone, turned back to the man, and said, "See? There's a friend of mine, and he's a photographer too. He's carrying a camera to prove it." He looked again at Eugene. "He doesn't believe I want to buy a camera. Tell him I'm a photographer too. He won't believe me."

The old man looked at Eugene. His hands stopped rummaging among the slips of paper. His eyes humbly begged for rescue. Very calmly, Eugene explained that he knew the boy. He apologized if he'd been any trouble. He also said he'd like to look at whatever cameras the man might have.

"Tell him I'm a photographer!" David demanded.

"Take it easy, will you?" said Eugene. The man, his arms limp at his sides, a sign of relief, shuffled toward a case filled with cameras.

"I told him I was a photographer and he didn't believe me!"

"Shut up, will you?"

David looked at him, astonished at this betrayal, then turned and went out of the shop, bumping against Mister Softee and slamming the door with such force that the jangling bells snarled rather than rang.

Eugene saw right away that his camera wasn't included in the display, and when he asked specifically for a 35-mm. Nikon, the man straightened up as much as he could. "I don't take anything that was stolen. I buy only from honest people." His hands began to tremble and Eugene tried to deny that he was looking for anything stolen, but the man obviously knew better. He almost sobbed with anger. Eugene tried to calm him by showing an interest in one of the better cameras, but it was snatched from his hands and he was ordered from the shop.

Eugene was even prepared to buy the camera. It

was one he could use, a replacement for the Nikon, and the price marked on it was better than reasonable. But the man refused to sell. Eugene stood silently, hoping he was giving the man a chance to vent the rest of his rage so he'd be calm after he was gone, but the man was now stamping his foot, weakly, and raising a trembling finger heavenward. Eugene thought it best to just leave. Before the door closed behind him, he heard the old man say, quietly, "If you come back in a day or two, I might have what you're looking for."

Outside, David was sitting on the stone step. "Why didn't you tell him I was a photographer?"

"You're not a photographer," said Eugene.

"What difference does it make? Now he thinks I'm a liar."

Eugene took him by the sleeve and began leading him away from the shop. David was wearing yesterday's Easter suit with the same shirt and the same canary-yellow tie. Only now the shirt cuffs fell out over his hands from the sleeves of the suit, the tie was askew and the suit itself rumpled, as though it had been slept in, fitfully. The shirt collar was wrinkled and soiled around the edge. A button was missing from the jacket. What looked like a tomato stain spotted the front of the shirt, and the spot's uneven edges, fading into a smudge, showed that an effort had been made to remove it. The shirt was half pulled out of the pants, and a belt, too large for David's skinny waist, dangled down sideways like a puppy dog's tongue. The tomato stain repeated itself just below the boy's left eye and on the lobe of his right ear. His lips apparently had been licked clean.

The idea of dragging David along with him did not appeal to Eugene. "Why don't you," he suggested lightly, hoping to avoid any hint of rejection that would, in turn, excite the boy to insistence, "why don't you hit a place I heard is over on Avenue B? I'll go down to Canal Street and then we can check with each other later."

"No, I better stay with you. And they'd pay better attention to me if I was the one wearing the camera."

For David to carry the camera was unthinkable. Loss, theft, breakage, all passed instantly before Eugene's pained eyes. David, knowing his fears, immediately promised he would not lose it, he would not break it, he would not let it get stolen. Nor would he take any pictures, a possibility Eugene had forgotten to consider. Now, however, he knew that David, given the camera, would very definitely take pictures.

They stood on the corner haggling. Finally a compromise was reached. But when Eugene thought back over the process by which it had been arranged, he was confronted by a hopeless tangle. All he knew was that they would both go to Canal Street *and* to Avenue B, together, and that David would "wear" the camera.

Without looking now at Saul Lorenzo, Eugene continued murmuring his interest, about to begin his refusal, when there was a clatter of falling objects in the next aisle and the sound of a sudden intake of breath.

"What's going on over there?" called Mr. Lorenzo.

"It's only me," they heard David say.

Eugene followed Mr. Lorenzo, squeezing between the display cases to the next aisle. They saw no one.

"Where are you?" Mr. Lorenzo was getting frantic.

David stood up from behind a display case. "I'm picking 'em up." He disappeared again.

"What're you doing back there?" Mr. Lorenzo now sounded frightened.

David stood up again when Eugene and Mr. Lorenzo came behind the cases. He was slowly wiping his left hand on his shirt, staining it with a blurred wash of blood. "I dropped one, and when I tried to catch it, they all fell."

At his feet lay a pile of knives and switchblades looking like sticks laid for a bonfire. David bent down again and continued to pick them up with his right hand.

"That case was locked. You broke it open. What're you two guys? Some racket together? I'm going to call the cops. Get away from there. Don't touch another one. Stand back or I go for the gun! Get away." He shooed David wildly, flapping his hands the way Eugene's grandmother would chase chickens out of her gladiola garden.

"I was only looking at 'em, and besides, the case wasn't locked. Look for yourself."

"You're dripping all over 'em. Get away." Mr. Lorenzo stooped down and began to pick them up, first tapping each switchblade with the tip of his forefinger to make sure it wouldn't spring open in his hand.

Pushing David out of the door ahead of him, Eugene heard Mr. Lorenzo call to him. "You want the camera? It's an excellent instrument."

Eugene wanted to take David to his mother's, or to Daniel's, where the cut could be washed and given a decent dressing, but the boy insisted no one was home either place and they didn't have anything there to bandage it with anyway. He suggested they go to Eugene's, but Eugene said they should go to the rectory, where the cut could be given the right kind of care.

David then told Eugene he knew a place he could go to and get it taken care of, but Eugene would have to come along. It was on Ninth Street, near Avenue C, and Eugene had to promise he'd tell no one anything about it. Eugene, wary, agreed.

When they got as far as the church, they saw men dressed in dark suits standing at the foot of the steps. Another clump of people, more colorfully dressed, hovered near the main entrance. Eugene hadn't realized. Today was Johnny's funeral.

As he started to take the camera from its pouch hanging from David's shoulder, the boy said, "What about my cut hand?"

"This'll only take a minute."

"It's still bleeding."

"Wrap your tie tighter around it."

The doors of the church opened and Eugene saw the silvery coffin come toward him. But, as he raised the camera, it was not the coffin that attracted his attention. Even in the dark of the church, he could see flashes of red and gold along the coffin's sides as it was being borne up the middle aisle. With the exception of one man in mufti, the pallbearers were wearing their Roman soldier costumes, complete with breastplates, sandals, and crested helmets.

When the cortege emerged into the light of the church steps, Eugene saw that Raimundo was, of course, one of the pallbearers, the last on the left, so he could carry the coffin with his good hand. His eye patch was gone and the few stitches gave an even greater fullness to the eyebrow. Like those of the other soldiers, his breastplate and helmet showed signs of mending, and even at a distance Eugene could see that only the repaired places had received a new coating of golden paint.

"They don't want you to take pictures." David practically hissed the words. Eugene clicked the shutter and Raimundo blinked.

Father Carusone moved to the front of the coffin, flanked by two altar boys. Eugene had to step to one side to get a second picture of Raimundo. Through the viewer he saw, behind Raimundo, Johnny's mother, the woman he had tried to warn away from the riot. She was wearing, not the worn slippers or the house dress now, but shoes of shining black laced up the front, and a black silk dress. On her head was a black lace mantilla flowing down over her shoulders, graceful and beautiful. She was supported by a young girl in a buttercup-yellow dress, and a middle-aged man whom Eugene recognized as the one who had carried the cross.

Watching the coffin pass by, Eugene thought: There's Johnny, lying inside. In his soldier costume? Eugene expected at least a touch of grief to return, but there came instead a sorrow over the loss, not of Johnny, but of the peace and comfort his grief for Johnny had given him. It seemed as though he had been allowed that brief quiet moment as a respite before this whole fresh clutter that was rattling around him now. He had thought the death of Johnny released him from the neighborhood, as he had thought losing the camera had released him, but here he was, back again, taking pictures of Raimundo, the boy at his side, watching poor abandoned Johnny himself being carted by in a silver coffin. Freedom seemed far off.

Raimundo passed in front of him. Eugene saw that the crest of his helmet was still creased along one side about the length of a Coca-Cola bottle. Eyes front, Raimundo did not look at Eugene or at the camera, but he knew they were there. The camera clicked again and then again.

As Eugene was about to put the camera back into the pouch, Johnny's mother, being led to the limousine reserved for the immediate family, stopped just before passing Father Carusone. Throwing her head back so that the mantilla fell to her shoulders, she began flailing the priest with her purse. Spitting out words in Spanish, she hit him again and again. The young girl at her side screamed and began to cry. She tugged at her mother's arm. The man yelled at both the mother and the girl.

The undertaker stepped up professionally and tried to take the mother's elbow and continue her toward the waiting car, but she pulled away from him, the mantilla now hanging from one shoulder only.

Father Carusone reached out a hand, not so much to stop the woman as to calm her. He spoke quietly in Spanish as the woman hit him again, and this time the strap of her purse caught on his outstretched hand. Seeing the purse dangling there as though he had snatched it from her, she reared back and screamed, pointing at the priest and at the purse, as if asking her fellow mourners to witness the theft.

Eugene began raising the camera, but before he could take the picture, Johnny's mother had grabbed at the purse, undoing the clasp, so that when she pulled it toward her a shower of coins, some wilted khaki-colored envelopes, and a fresh lace handkerchief spilled out onto the sidewalk.

Immediately her screaming stopped. She stretched out her arms, bowed her head, and viewed her worldly goods in an attitude almost of prayerful silence.

Father Carusone knelt down to pick up the coins, the envelopes, and the handkerchief. Again Eugene began to raise the camera, but stopped. Johnny's mother had drawn the head of the kneeling priest to her breast, and bending over it, she began a rocking movement, smoothing with her hands the ruffled hair.

The man who had carried the cross, and some of the other mourners, took over the task of retrieving the purse's contents, as Father Carusone, still kneeling, gently pulled free of the woman's arms and looked up at her. With his open hand he wiped the woman's cheeks. She remained still, obediently letting him do it, then helped to raise him up. She said only, *"Mi cartera."* David translated for Eugene. It meant "my purse."

The purse was handed to her. She opened it, checked the contents, nodded, snapped it shut, put the mantilla back on her head, and held out one arm to the girl and the other to the man. Her expression of grief returned and she got into the limousine as though nothing had stayed her steps since she had come from the church, chief mourner for the meanest man Father Carusone had ever met.

The limousine, the hearse, the cars drove off.

Eugene had let it all happen without photographing it, except for those few pictures of Raimundo. While zipping the camera back into the pouch, he saw a dime on the sidewalk, the only remaining sign of all that had happened. David saw it, too, and started toward it.

"Leave it there!" Even Eugene was startled by the fury of his command.

"Why should I—" David began, as he leaned down.

"I said leave it there!" He straightened David up and held out the pouch. "Here, take this so we can get going. You're still bleeding."

After they had turned the corner onto Ninth Street, David asked, "Why couldn't I have the dime?"

"Why do I have to know why? Why do I have to know anything! Just leave me alone."

David, for a change, said nothing.

9

The building David took Eugene to had smoke stains on the outside that rose from the second- and third-floor windows like hair standing on end in fright. The entire tenement looked as though it had been burned out. The windows and the front entrance had been sealed with sheets of tin, and to get inside, David led Eugene into the building next door, up to the roof, across to the fire escape, and in through a bathroom window where the tin had been loosened and could be bent back.

The window itself was broken, frame and all. The solid windowless wall of a warehouse about ten feet from the back of the building protected them from curious neighbors. The toilet in the bathroom where they entered was running, gurgling like a brook.

"Don't worry about the stairs being safe," David

whispered. "The fire didn't come up this side. Just the smoke and the water from the hoses. Where we're going is down on the next floor."

The windows in the hallway let onto an air shaft, and through their grime all outside light was transmuted into shadow. Since the electricity had been turned off, Eugene and David moved slowly down the stairs in near darkness. The after-smell of smoke was cleansing and cool.

"Is it still bleeding?" asked Eugene.

"I can't tell. My tie stopped it, I think."

At the bottom of the one flight of stairs David said, "This here is it. I know where the candles are." He stepped through an opening where the door had been splintered and wrenched off its hinges. "The firemen did that," explained David. "Wait here till I light candles so you can see."

Waiting in the hall, Eugene listened for other sounds. He heard nothing except the distant gurgling of the upstairs toilet and the street noises, echoing far off like sounds coming at dusk from the other side of a lake.

A match was struck. A glow filled the center of the room, stretched itself, then reached into the corners as David lit a second, then a third candle. "There are windows on the air shaft," David said, "but I want you to see what it's really like. Come on in."

Eugene stepped into the room. The walls, from ceiling to floor, were streaked with stains of water and smoke, gray and amber runnels, as though some gigantic weeping had happened here. Above a mantel directly opposite the door, a sooted mirror reflected Eugene standing there, webbed in shadows, half hidden by smoke. Under the tin-sealed windows that probably faced the street, a plush couch, bedraggled and matted, stood dumbly like an enormous cow that had been rescued too late from the pond. Near it, like a sodden calf, was a matching chair, and next to it a round table whose warped veneer top reminded him of the crinkly serrations of Helen's hair.

All other furniture, salvageable perhaps, had been removed, making what remained look that much more abandoned and forlorn. A scuffed suitcase in front of the couch suggested a coffee table and it was there that one of the candles burned. Another burned on a kitchen chair placed just outside an alcove at the other end of the room, away from the windows. The back of the chair had been broken off.

In the alcove itself was a bed partly covered by a worn and rumpled rug thrown over a stained mattress. A single pillow was protected by a fairly clean white towel, which Eugene thought he recognized as one of his own. A depression in the middle of the pillow suggested that someone had slept there.

At the foot of the bed were the corduroy pants, the T-shirt, and the jacket David had been wearing before. One sneaker was near the bed, the other on the chair next to the candle. Socks and undershorts littered the floor, along with an empty Fig Newton box, some candy wrappers, and the tray from a TV dinner. An apple and an unopened Twinkie were on the windowsill, and outside on the ledge was a quart bottle of Pepsi, half empty.

David lit a fourth candle in the trough of two serrations on the tabletop. "It was a little wet at first, but feel, it's all dried now. Not even damp. I build a fire once in a while. In the fireplace. But only after it's dark, so no one can see the smoke, or I'd build you one now. There's still two chairs in the kitchen I can burn, and I brought up some dresser drawers I got under the bed. The dresser's too big, though, for all by myself."

"You live here?"

"I come here once in a while."

"There isn't any Daniel?"

"Sure. He's in my grade."

"You never stay with his family, though."

"Want to see the apartment where the people died? It wasn't even where the fire started. Two guys and this girl. Right across the hall."

"Go wash your hand. I want to see how bad the cut is."

Going toward a door to the left of the alcove, David picked up a sock and put it on the half chair. With his foot, he slid the TV-dinner tray under the bed. "Seven firemen were hospitalized for smoke inhalation," said David, newspaper-style. "They were treated and released on their own recognizance."

Taking the candle from the chair, he left the room, and soon Eugene heard running water. He picked up what he guessed was the matching sock, put it on the chair, and followed the sound.

The kitchen was bare except for the two chairs, one of which had fallen over for want of a fourth leg. What light there was came through the dirty air-shaft windows, which had not been tinned. Here the walls were a striped amber that looked like hardened glue, as though the fire had melted decades of grease soaked into the plaster, drawing it out like fat from a roasting goose. Congealed by the water of the firemen's hose and squeezed into rivulets by the water coursing through from the apartment above, it stuck to the walls, waiting perhaps for a future warmth that would allow it to complete its downward flow. Again, the after-smell of smoke was cleansing, as though the fire had burned up all the impurities and left behind this autumn odor, cool and fresh.

In the corner of an otherwise empty cupboard, a can of sardines in tomato sauce, two cans of ravioli, and a box of Ritz crackers huddled together as if for warmth. Two greasy plates, a cup, and some stained silverware littered the bottom of the sink like the exposed refuse in a drained swamp.

"I'm hardly cut at all. It just bled a little."

In the cramped, closet-sized bathroom, Eugene took the hand and looked down at the wound. It cut across the palm, a dark red thread, intersecting all the lines of life and love and fate. He pressed gently on either side of the cut, testing to see if the bleeding had really stopped. David looked at him, then at his hand. In the light of the single candle, Eugene might have been a gypsy palmist, studying for hints of what lay in wait for the boy.

"What were you going to steal a knife for?" Without looking at David, Eugene continued to prod the hand gently to see if it would bleed again.

"I was only looking."

"You ever have a knife?"

"Sure. But they always take it away."

"Ever use one?"

"Sure." Eugene looked up at him. "Carving trees, and once in a while you slash a tire."

"Ever cut anybody?"

"In the seventh grade. They sent me home."

Eugene slowly closed the hand into a fist, then slowly opened it. The line moistened a little as some blood surfaced, but there was no flow.

"When was the last time you had one?"

"Christmas. Father took it away before school even started again."

Eugene took out a clean, unironed handkerchief and dabbed at the wound lightly. "How long you been living here?"

David shrugged but said nothing.

Eugene wrapped the handkerchief around the hand and knotted it with a double knot. "Too tight?"

"Use my tie. It's already got blood on it."

"It's dirty."

"It's brand-new for Easter."

Eugene pressed the handkerchief lightly, but no

blood came through. "Try not to use the hand for a while, and be sure you wash it again later."

Looking at the bandage, David kept opening and closing his hand as if he wanted to see how often he could do it without making it bleed again.

"Don't, dummy."

The boy stopped and just looked at the handkerchief. Nothing seeped through. When he looked up at Eugene, he seemed to be preparing himself to say thanks, but he said instead, "You want to piss?"

"Thanks, I don't have to," said Eugene. He went back to the living room. David followed.

"You don't have to go right away," he said.

"I have to work."

"In your darkroom?"

"Yeah."

"Why don't you stay and I'll make us some sardines?"

Eugene, out of habit, started to refuse, but he stopped himself before the natural no came out. "Okay," he said. "I could eat a sardine, I guess." Then he remembered to add, "Thanks."

David was surprised. "You really want some?"

"I guess so. Why not?"

"Sit over on the couch and I'll fix 'em. Take the Pepsi with you."

As they ate, the boy became quiet, and Eugene, for a change, felt obliged to make conversation. "Would you believe I never ate a sardine before?"

The boy looked at him as though curious why he

had to tell such an insignificant lie. "They're good," said David, ignoring what Eugene had said. "Eat another one."

"I guess," explained Eugene, "I guess in Iowa we've got so much fresh stuff—meat, I mean, and vegetables—it never occurred to my grandmother to buy a can of sardines."

David put another sardine onto Eugene's plate but said nothing.

"Did you know I grew up on a farm? My grandparents'. My grandmother and my grandfather. On my mother's side. Outside a town called Atlantis. After the lost continent. You know about the lost continent?"

David nodded. "In a comic book." And there the conversation ended.

The silence unsettled Eugene. He didn't know what he was doing there in the first place. He had expected endless chatter. Without it, without a cause for exasperation, he had no ready emotion to direct toward the boy. He had tried condescension with the sardines and hadn't been believed. Autobiography got him nowhere. The boy, for whatever reason, had become shy again. Exploring with his eyes different parts of the room as though *he* were the guest, David ate without looking at his companion. He would chew and swallow, chew and swallow. The scar on his cheek wriggled, doing a little dance, then waited patiently for another bite to set it in motion again. David reached for the box of crackers and looked inside. He meted out two crackers for himself and two for Eugene. That emptied the box.

"I don't want any more," said Eugene.

David put the two crackers back into the box, placing them carefully on the bottom so they wouldn't break or crumble. He looked down into the box as though counting them, making sure they were both there. Then he set the box down next to him.

"You want some help carrying that dresser up from downstairs?" asked Eugene after a lengthy silence.

"You don't have to help. I'm all right."

"No, let me. You want it, you might as well have it." He dripped tomato sauce down the front of his shirt, scooped it up on his finger, and licked it off. He expected the boy to laugh. The boy made no sound at all.

As they brought the dresser up the stairs, David found his tongue again. Eugene was told about the three people who had died in the fire, they were junkies, and the old woman who had run back into the burning building to get her sewing machine. He was told about the two dogs that had been rescued by firemen on ladders and how the rubber bags looked with three dead people inside. Bragging slightly, David said he had no rats, they'd all died in the fire, mostly killed by smoke in the basement.

There was also a lecture on the difference between sardines in tomato sauce and sardines in oil, advice on karate, admonitions not to get his clothes dirty by rubbing up against the walls, and, of course, repeated directions on how to carry a dresser up the stairs.

When the dresser was placed against the wall next to the fireplace, David ran back downstairs and returned with a blue glass vase, which he put on top.

"You going to burn the dresser or use it?" asked Eugene.

"I don't know yet."

Eugene picked up the camera pouch, ready to go. "Thanks for the sardines."

David shrugged again. "You never had them before." He began to examine his bandaged palm, now slightly stained with both blood and tomato sauce. "You don't have to go, you don't want to," he said.

"I told you. I have to work. But thanks for lunch."

David dismissed it with a quick hunch of his shoulders. "You helped with the dresser." He had become quiet again. He ran a single finger over the bandage as though a little confused that his hand should have this strange texture. "I don't suppose you changed your mind about me coming to help."

"I never let anyone in the darkroom when I'm working," he lied.

The boy, still examining the bandage, nodded, accepting the refusal.

"You going to stay here now?" asked Eugene.

David went and blew out the candle on the suitcase. "Maybe for a little while." Just before snuffing out the candle on the chair next to the bed, he said, "We don't need these now you know how it looks."

The last one he blew out was on the mantel, extinguishing at the same time Eugene's mottled image in the sooted glass. With the lessening of the light, Eugene became aware again of street sounds, still way off, far away.

David continued to study the bandage knot on the back of his hand, picking at it with his thumb and forefinger. Eugene turned to go.

"Wait!" said David.

"What for? What's wrong?"

"I . . . I only thought maybe I should check in the camera pouch to make sure everything's all there."

"Why shouldn't it all be there?"

David hesitated, then went to him, opened the pouch, and took out a small but intricate-looking transistor radio.

"How'd that get in there?" asked Eugene.

David looked at the radio, then flipped it on.

"You swiped it," said Eugene. "One of the hock shops. When?"

Music blared out. David turned the sound lower, then switched stations until a voice was heard talking. Without looking up at Eugene, he said, "It gets so quiet sometimes."

10

What had looked to Eugene like a clinic last Saturday was now something of a combination meeting room and waiting room for Father Carusone's office. No one was there except Eugene, and after he'd been sitting for about five minutes, he realized his chair was the one where Mr. Economu had sat to get his foot washed. Through the office door Eugene could hear low murmurings and long silences. He shifted his legs nervously, crossing the calf of one across the knee of the other, then reversing the position. Next he crossed his ankles, then sat upright, with both feet flat on the floor.

Priests made him uneasy. They had all that power and, besides, they knew too much about you.

The office door opened and a girl of about seven-

teen and a man, or a boy, of about the same age came
out ahead of Father Carusone. The girl and the boy
were holding hands as if for mutual protection, looking
like Hansel and Gretel just after all the bread crumbs
had disappeared. The girl turned back toward the priest
and whispered, "Thank you, Father."

"Eugene!" The priest recognized him and remembered his name. In contrast to the young people, Father
Carusone seemed extremely cheerful. "This is Kathy
and this is Tony. They're getting married. This is
Eugene."

"Congratulations," said Eugene. Instead of holding
out his hand, which would require them to separate, he
bowed a low bow as if in homage to their courage. They
smiled weakly and nodded back as though not sure what
the priest had meant when he said "married," then went
out, looking, as far as Eugene could see, as though they
would never, never find their way home through the
dark forest.

"Sorry. Nothing about the camera," said the priest
to Eugene rather abruptly.

"That's not why I'm here."

Father Carusone looked at his watch. "I'm late for
the hospital. We still have two people from Saturday.
And one in jail. Walk me out to the car, can you?"

Eugene almost used this as an excuse to just turn
and go, but he held fast to his reason for being there.
"You don't have a minute?" he said, surprised by the
pleading note in his voice.

"How important is it?"

"I . . . I don't know."

"Then let's find out." Father Carusone sat down, took off his glasses, balanced them on his knee, then rubbed his face with the flat palms of his hands as though scrubbing it clean. The glasses fell to the floor and he picked them up before Eugene had even started to bend down. When he put the glasses back on, he looked as though he'd just waked up, refreshed and ready for what lay ahead. "Tell me."

"First of all, I apologize if I butted in at the funeral, taking those pictures."

Father Carusone waved his hand quickly, impatiently, but still agreeing. "Good. Sorry. Okay. Then what?"

Eugene felt he was back in confession, with the priest encouraging him to get to the heart of the matter. "You know," said Eugene, "that kid was with me today, David Stokes? I asked you for his address last Saturday when I thought he was the one stole my camera?"

The priest stood up as though what Eugene had said put an end to the interview. "Oh. David. Please." He raised both hands as if in surrender.

"You know all about him?"

"I don't know all about anybody," he said, contradicting Eugene's general notion about priests, "but what I do know about David . . . well . . . Now what?"

"You know he doesn't live with his family?"

"Walk me to the car. I'm late." They started out. Going down the outside steps, Father Carusone said,

———————

"What family? Living with them would be like living in a nuthouse."

"I met them," said Eugene. "Briefly. His mother and the man who takes care of them."

"The car's around the corner. Keep talking."

"You know he's not living with them?"

"Yup. And I know he's not living with the Costellos."

"That the Daniel his mother thinks he's with?"

"She knows he's not there any more. And I know he's not there any more. I also know he's not at the children's shelter, because he ran away twice, and I also know he's not at St. Michael's, and I also know he's not at Rockledge, and he's not at the Detention Center. In other words, I know all the places he's not. But no, I don't know the place where he is, and I'm not sure I want to."

"Oh?" It surprised Eugene. He had grown up assuming that a priest would promptly solve any problem brought to him.

They reached the car. "I don't like to take up problems when I know they don't have a solution." At least he'd explained his unusual reaction to David's situation. "Or at least," the priest went on, "one I can come up with. But keep talking."

"He's staying in a burned-out tenement, one of the apartments, over on Ninth Street. I was just there."

"I'd been wondering. Now I know." He started to take off his glasses, but changed his mind. "Is he eating, do you know?"

"Canned stuff, TV dinners, Coke. I think he gets money from his mother to give to . . . that family . . . the Costellos?"

"No heat, no running water, I suppose."

"The water's on."

"What about heat? It still gets cold."

"The fireplace works. There's furniture left behind. He burns it."

"You have to give him credit for being resourceful, don't you? What about rats?"

"He says they all died in the fire. Mostly smoke. In the basement, he said."

"Then what's the problem?"

Eugene was amazed. "Can he live there like that?"

"Looks like he can." Father Carusone opened the car door.

"But with no real food, no real heat. Alone, dirty, all smoked up, greasy. How long can he stay there like that?"

"I don't know." The priest blew out a long breath and leaned one elbow on the roof of the car.

"And what," said Eugene, "what if some junkies or who knows who decide they want to move in? Or suppose David goes there and somebody's there who doesn't like being interrupted when he's shooting up or something?"

Off came the glasses and again Father Carusone scrubbed his face, but this time he did not seem refreshed. "Why don't you let him live with you?" he asked.

"Me?"

"Let him live with you. You got a spare couch? Or a corner? A nook? A cranny? An empty cupboard, maybe? I've asked everybody else and now I'm asking you. I can't take him because the rectory's filled up. The old pastor is still here and I've got an alcoholic and an ex-seminarian, both of them suffering from withdrawal symptoms. You've got a place, haven't you? You take him." He got into the car and slid over to the driver's seat. Eugene poked his head in the door before the priest could close it.

"I . . . I can't take him. I . . . I just can't."

"Then that settles it, doesn't it?"

"Can't you find anybody who cares?"

"Lots of people care. I care. I care, I care, I care." The priest put his elbow on the steering wheel and leaned his forehead onto his hand. "Some days I think all I'm good for is caring. That there's nothing else I can really do. What should I try with the kid? Have him locked up behind bars so he can't get away?" He shook his head and shuddered as if warding off just the idea. Putting the key into the ignition, he looked straight ahead through the windshield. "You don't want him? You can't take him? Believe me when I tell you I don't have one more single suggestion in my head." He started the motor. "But don't feel too bad about it. The kid probably wouldn't want to stay with you, anyway. Say a prayer." He let out a long breath, a weary "whooo," as though reflecting with a sad wisdom that this particular solution carried few guarantees.

(145

"Slam the door, huh? I'm late. David. David Stokes." He stared at his hands on the steering wheel as if wondering what they were doing there. Then he gunned the motor. Eugene shut the door, but it didn't catch. As the car moved off, he ran alongside, opening the door again and giving it a good slam.

As the car sped away, a fat woman walking a dog shouted and waved a greeting, then crossed the street, talking to the waddling dog, explaining proudly that the priest, "the father," had just crossed their path.

11

When the bell clanged in the loft that night, Eugene was sure it was Raimundo. The funeral pictures were developed and those of Raimundo enlarged and printed. The others he and Raimundo would print together in the darkroom, the two of them. That, at least, was Eugene's plan.

And the darkroom, he figured, would work very well. What it offered, he sensed, was ambiguity. The accidental touch wouldn't have to be explained; the size of the room, the essential activities excused it, if an excuse was necessary. There could be explorations back and forth, an uncertain closeness, a touch lingering perhaps beyond its need. Does one move or stay? All signposts would have to be interpreted rather than simply read. Success would hover like an impatient angel; nothing would be certain.

But it was the "differentness" of the room itself that promoted the most helpful ambiguity of all. Not without reason does the seducer favor the out-of-the-way place, the unusual setting. A sense of the secret helps, but there's more to it than that. In the darkroom, for instance, the paraphernalia, the unfamiliar forms, the shapes lighted only by the red safelight, the overall feeling that something mysterious happens here, all this could easily effect a sense of remove: in such surroundings, one is not oneself. Or so one can always claim.

Relieved of the ordinary, cast into the exotic, a different self is suggested. Experiment is encouraged, the possibilities excite, and protection is provided automatically.

The touch lingers longer, the closeness, the pressure of the arm, the thigh, the placement of the hand, the slight pull, closer. A pact is reached, permissions exchanged, with no word spoken. The walls of the room thrust the body's emanations back toward itself, multiplying all intensities. Nothing is known, not the self, not the surrounding world, not the destination or the road up ahead.

A beating of wings is heard, the hovering angel descends, thrashing the air.

Again the bell rang out. Eugene threw open the window, a greeting ready for Raimundo. There on the sidewalk, David held up what looked like a bottle of

148)

Pepsi-Cola. He'd done it before and here he was doing it again, substituting himself for Raimundo!

"I'm working!" Eugene called down. "And what are you doing here anyway?"

David smiled up at him, holding the bottle over his head. "I've got some wine."

"I said I'm working!"

David held the bottle higher. "It's for you."

"Didn't you hear me? I don't want it."

The smile left David's face and he stared up at Eugene as though he hadn't heard. He was not ignoring the rejection, he simply had no comprehension of what it meant. He decided to start all over again. Holding the bottle up by the neck, like something he'd caught hunting, he shouted cheerfully, "I've got some wine!"

Eugene started to slam the window down, but he knew the boy would be back, pulling on the bell, holding up the bottle and calling, "I've got some wine." The only way to get rid of him was to tell him specifically not to keep coming around, that he, Eugene, did not want the wine, that he didn't need his help in the darkroom, that he, David, was a royal pain in the ass.

Vowing to say exactly that, without elaboration or distraction, Eugene called down, "Okay. The door's unlocked. Come on up."

Eugene could tell by the pacing on the stairs that the steps were being taken two at a time. There was a stumble after the third landing, then a silence. When it lasted more than a few seconds, Eugene opened the door to see if the boy was hurt.

David bounded up the last few steps and bounced into the room, laughing. The laughter had a mockery mixed into it, as though he were taunting Eugene for inviting him into the loft, after all.

"What the hell are you doing here, anyway?" Eugene wanted to sound even angrier than he did. He also wanted to say the one thing he knew he couldn't say, that he had no help to offer him, that, like Father Carusone, he had no solution for his situation and didn't like to be reminded of it. That was the real reason Eugene was angry, but he couldn't bring himself to admit it out loud, especially to David himself. "I told you I'd be working." Now he sounded angrier.

"I saw him! On the stairs!" David was jubilant.

"Saw who on the stairs?"

"He was eating something. It looked like a raisin."

"Are you drunk?"

Reminded why he had come, David held out the wine bottle. "I brought us some wine so we could drink it."

"There's no one on the stairs."

"I scared him when I stumbled. He left his raisin on the step."

Eugene closed the door. He spoke with slow deliberateness. "There are no rats in this building."

David smiled eagerly. "Come on in the hallway. I'll show you the raisin."

"Will you stop coming around here all the time? I'm working. How many times do I have to tell you?"

"Oh," said David slowly, as though agreeing to give this strange concept his full consideration. He looked at Eugene as if hoping to get some help in realizing the implication of what had been said. Eugene stayed silent. David looked down at the wine bottle and began to pick at the label.

"Can't I watch? While you're working?" he asked quietly.

"No. Nobody can watch. I told you that." Because the boy had forced him to lie again, he was even more angry than before. He put his fists on his hips in mock patience, waiting for David to leave.

"You want me to come back later?" He stopped picking at the label and looked at Eugene.

"Don't you have any friends?" said Eugene, almost pleading for the boy himself to lie and say yes.

In answer, David shrugged, then glanced around the room. "I'm going to build myself a bed just like that one."

"Look," said Eugene, "you're a nice kid. I like you. But you can't come hanging around. You can understand that, can't you? I've got things I've just got to get done."

His mouth partly open, his eyebrows pinched in toward each other, David blinked three times, as though it would help him find the right response to what Eugene was saying. He turned away and went to the bed, examining, not the joinings or the engineering, but the grain of the wood. "I know where I can get wood just like this." He ran a finger up and down it slowly, as if the knowledge of how to build a loft bed could be absorbed by tactile means alone.

"You are not going to build a bed like that."

David continued to run the tips of his fingers along the boards, taking in the flow and pattern of the grain. "Except I'm going to build mine higher. Almost to the ceiling."

"You build it too high, it'll get stuffy and hot. And you'll bang your head."

"I won't hit my head." David turned and looked at Eugene. His voice had the tone of a quiet promise.

"Then you won't hit your head. But you've got to go. Okay?"

"My cut, it turned out not bad." David raised his hand, palm outward, the straight diagonal still bisecting the lines of life and love and fate, but dry now and lightly scabbed.

Ashamed that he hadn't even asked about the cut, but trying not to lose his impatience, Eugene said quickly, "Good. I'm glad."

"I'll bring you back your handkerchief when it's clean, okay?"

"Keep it. It—it's yours."

"Yeah?" David smiled, surprised, pleased at the generosity. Then, when Eugene offered nothing more on the subject of his injury, the boy began to pick casually at the plastic band that sealed the wine bottle.

"Don't open that."

"Didn't you really ever have a sardine before?"

Eugene grabbed the bottle and banged it down on the table next to the couch. "Go! Will you?!" He started to lead David to the door.

The bell rang out.

"You want me to tell who it is they should go away, you're working?" said David eagerly.

"No, you go on. I can do it." Eugene began to go back for the bottle but remembered he had forgotten to buy wine. "I'll pay you for the wine. How much was it?"

"Nothing," said David. He opened the door. "Let me tell who it is you're working. Okay?" He asked it as though it were a supreme favor.

Heavy clumping was heard on the stairs. "Don't come up," David called. "He's got to work."

"Come on up," said Eugene.

David started to turn toward Eugene to correct him, to remind him of what he'd obviously forgotten, but he stopped. He studied the floor a moment, then raised his head slowly. Without looking at Eugene, he started down the long flight of stairs, half skipping, his hair flopping up and down. Only once did he stop, and that was to jerk the hair back from his eyes. He passed Raimundo just above the third-floor landing. Raising his head a little higher, he jerked the hair from his eyes once more.

Raimundo moved to the center of the steps, blocking the boy from Eugene's view. Eugene didn't see him go, only heard the skipping sound receding down the stairs.

"You got a lot of steps," Raimundo called, waving his cast.

"Sorry."

Raimundo began puffing, not because he was out of breath, but because he seemed to think it would amuse. It did. "Who's been eating raisins?" he asked.

"What?"

Raimundo stopped on the stairs and gave a harsh "aaah" as he ground something into the step with the toe of his shoe. When he reached the top, he said casually, "That kid, watch out for him. He is a faggot."

Eugene heard the downstairs door close. He tried to laugh, but it came out a snort. "Cut it out, will you? He is not." He tried to laugh again but with little more success.

Raimundo shrugged. "He is a faggot." Smiling a little, he clumped Eugene on the shoulder with his cast. "Did you take my picture this morning?" He walked into the room, obviously pleased to be there again.

"Yeah," said Eugene. "I got a couple." He paused, then asked, "Why did you say that about the kid?"

Raimundo shrugged again. "He is a faggot." He clapped his good hand against his cast like a baseball catcher encouraging the pitcher to make the pitch. "The pictures, did they turn out? I told Reina, I told her you took some more. She wants one. Saturday is her birthday. I got her a brush and a mirror and a comb, very beautiful. She'll show them to you before she uses them." He looked around the room. "Where are they, the pictures?" As though Eugene would have them hanging on the walls.

"I'll get them." Eugene went into the darkroom. Barely hearing Raimundo chatter something about the cemetery, he shuffled the pictures in his hands. He wished Raimundo had not said that about David. Even more, he wished David hadn't held his head so high when he left, or hadn't stopped on the stairs to jerk the hair back from his eyes.

Only vaguely did Eugene hear Raimundo say, "We were just getting ready to go, and Father, he was about to throw some dirt, then Gregory, he takes off his helmet and throws it down on top of the coffin. At first we thought it was the wind."

Eugene was thinking of David, but trying not to. Too many questions with unacceptable answers kept coming into his mind. Had the boy been pursuing him, trying in his own clumsy way to seduce him? Was *that* what all the intrusions were about? Eugene didn't want to even consider it. He forced himself to listen more closely to what the voice in the next room was saying.

"But when Gregory, he didn't jump down to get it back, Joey, he threw his helmet in, too."

Eugene decided that Raimundo was making up a story to amuse him, like the pretended puffing on the stairs, a performance intended to please. He also convinced himself that what Raimundo had said about David was one more fanciful lie, an extravagance offered to create interest, essentially harmless and not to be taken seriously. It had no more validity, Eugene decided, than the recipe for chili or the promise of a motorcycle ride. Or the story of the helmets, just concluded.

"Joey," he heard Raimundo say, "Joey is the one Johnny tried to run over with his uncle's Eldorado last Tuesday."

Eugene was now able to concentrate on the pictures. A full-length shot of the pallbearers and the coffin, with Raimundo's cast showing, proving he was able to do his part of the job with only one good hand—this picture Eugene placed on top. For the last, in the most favored place, he chose one of Raimundo from the shoulders up, alone, the crest of his helmet slanting back in the wind. His expression was one of utter passivity, no feature marred by emotion or distorted by thought. It had been taken as Johnny's mother began beating Father Carusone with her purse, and Eugene reflected that one of the advantages of photography was the opportunity to separate the subject from the predicate.

"Next year," Raimundo was saying, "next year, my woman, she will have to make me a new helmet, but it's all right. She had to make another one anyway, because it was all beat up in the procession. That's why I didn't mind throwing it into Johnny's grave like Joey and Gregory. It was like throwing garbage into the garbage can. Right?"

Eugene went into the living room. Raimundo was sitting contentedly in the rocking chair. In his good hand was a glass of wine and, just as Eugene entered, he was taking a good long gulp. The sugar bowl was next to the bottle.

Eugene held out the pictures, saying, "They're not as good as I hoped they'd be," knowing the opposite was true.

Raimundo stood up and took the pictures. Looking at them, he seemed almost awed. "Oh, they are very good." He looked at another one. "Very good." And another. "Oh, that is very good."

Shuffling the prints slowly, looking longer each time at each one, he let out "ooohs" and "aaahs," sometimes snorting affectionate approval, sometimes gazing with rapt admiration. In the guise of praising the photographer, he was allowed to appreciate to the fullest his own image.

Narcissism, Eugene realized as he watched him, had more than its share of virtues. Raimundo was not vain, he was beyond vanity. Neither was he envious, nor greedy, and his demands on others were minimal. His self-admiration was unassailable and he assumed his worth was a knowledge shared by one and all. Good will came easily to him. He accepted friendships without suspicion, as he had accepted Eugene's friendship. Perhaps, thought Eugene, what the world needed was more narcissists, more Raimundos.

"Oh, they are beautiful. And I can have them?"

"Of course you can have them. And I thought maybe you'll help me print some others I took today. Then if you want any of those, you can have them too."

"You mean me work with you in the bathroom?"

"In the darkroom. Yeah."

"With only that red light on?" He sounded wary.

"That's the way we do the printing." Eugene hesitated, then went on. "Why?"

"If I tell you something, you won't tell anyone?"

"Of course not. What?"

Raimundo looked down at his picture, tracing with his finger the line of his profile. "With the red light on, I am afraid."

"How can you be afraid? You can see all right when it's on."

"Can't we work in the dark? With no light on at all?"

"But what's wrong with having the red light on? It's called a safelight. Why don't you like it?"

Raimundo rubbed what seemed to be a blemish on the picture of his chin. "The red light, it makes me think the devil is there," he said quietly.

"The devil?"

"The devil. I don't like it like that. We'll work in the dark. Then it won't make me afraid."

Eugene thought a moment. "All right," he said, "we'll work in the dark."

Raimundo went to the table and put down the pictures, gazing again at himself with his crest blown back in the wind.

"But first, before we print the pictures," said Eugene, "we'll have a glass of wine."

"Wine," said Raimundo, agreeing. "And you are my friend."

They both sipped. It was sticky and sweet. "This wine," said Raimundo, "they know how to make it right." He added only one spoon of sugar. "That kid," he said, "he was with you today at the funeral. But watch out for him. He begins to bother you, you tell me."

Eugene wanted to change the subject, but he wasn't quick enough.

"Once," said Raimundo, "you know what he did, that kid? Gregory told me last month he was painting his fire escape for the rent and the kid, he helped him for two days because you have to put first one coat on and then the second coat on. One night when Gregory's mother and his aunt, they went to bingo, the kid comes and brings him a bottle of wine. He must have stole it. He brought it to Gregory's and he made Gregory drink most of it. Then I won't tell you what happened."

"You're crazy," said Eugene. "And so is Gregory."

Raimundo took another sip of the wine. "Someday he will help you do something like he did Gregory and the fire escape, and then he will come with a bottle of wine and . . ." Raimundo paused and looked at the glass he was raising again to his lips. A thought seemed to flicker quickly like a lightning bug in his mind, but he immediately extinguished it. He took two more sips, looked again into his glass, and continued: ". . . then you have to be careful. Don't drink it when he brings it." He took a full gulp.

Eugene set his glass on the table and looked at his hand holding it. A vision of the boy, standing so joyfully on the sidewalk, holding up the bottle, came to his mind. "I've got some wine . . . It's for you!" Again Eugene forced himself to listen to what Raimundo was saying.

"I never drink wine. I always drink whiskey." Raimundo took another sip of the wine.

Eugene wanted to say nothing, but he knew silence was not allowed. "I drink wine. Beer when I was growing up."

Raimundo raised his glass, then suddenly slammed it down on the table, splashing wine on Eugene's hand. He jumped up, giving a loud, open-mouthed yell.

"What's wrong?" asked Eugene, not taking his hand from his glass.

Raimundo whipped his right arm across his body to his left side and brought the arm back again, raised now and reaching out. A quick click and Eugene saw a long slender blade like a single finger lengthened and forged into a steel instrument. Eugene did not move. Raimundo, bending slightly at the knees, crouched into a position of attack. His head moved in quick spasms as he looked now at the corners of the room, now at the floor, now at Eugene. Eugene said nothing.

Raimundo opened his mouth slightly. His breathing was deep and long, his lips quivering as he inhaled almost to a gasp and exhaled almost to a moan. The skin of his face was stretched taut, his eyes wide.

Eugene sat up straighter in his chair, not letting go of the glass. Raimundo held his breath, then the hand holding the blade began to rise slowly from his side. Suddenly he took three fast strides to the far side of the room, reared back, and plunged the knife down into the floor.

Quickly he pulled it out and stood up, half turning toward the darkroom door. He moved again, two steps, plunging the knife down, this time into the baseboard along the wall. He freed it from the wood and bent into an attack position again, the knife poised on a level with his thigh. Twice he slashed the air, a defiant invitation to combat.

Eugene was about to get up and move away when he heard a scratching sound and saw Raimundo turn toward him, rear back again, and bring the blade down full-force into the floor. He heard the long screech like a night bird crying out and he saw the rat leap up along the blade, forcing it through his entire body. A high gurgling sound came from Raimundo as though he, too, had been struck. Then Eugene saw him pull the knife away, raising the rat a full foot from the floor before it dropped from the blade and went scratching, squealing toward the wall of the darkroom.

Raimundo growled in his throat, then searched along the wall. He brought himself up onto the balls of his feet and put his bad hand behind him so it wouldn't get in the way. He took short fast steps, and coming down on both feet at the same time, he arched the knife into a downward thrust. The shriek came again, only this time half gargled in blood. There was no leap up onto the blade, but the rat stretched its neck and raised its head, touching the back of Raimundo's hand with its fur.

Raimundo leaned down to it, still pinned to the floor. "What? Huh?" he said, as though expecting the rat to speak up, to make its case, to plead its cause. "What?" Then, contemptuous of the rat's silence, he withdrew the blade, which, this time, was washed a watery pink.

Eugene stood up. "I'll go get a newspaper."

"No! Not yet." Raimundo stooped down to the rat again. The rat was now rumbling in place, its feet scurrying underneath it but unable to carry it anywhere. Or perhaps it was trying to cuddle itself into a more comfortable position for death.

"You got it," said Eugene. "Now leave it alone. Let me go get a newspaper." He started toward the kitchen.

Raimundo continued to nag the rat. "What? Go on. What?" He nudged it with the tip of the blade. The hunched body pulled itself in closer from the cold touch of the steel. Raimundo started to stand up, perhaps to lunge again, but before he straightened himself, the rat leaped two feet up into the air, almost slapping Raimundo's chin. With the blade, Raimundo caught it on its side, flinging it away from the wall, out into the middle of the room. It clawed the floor but, finding it couldn't move, stayed perfectly still, flicking its ears.

"Don't touch it any more." But Raimundo moved toward the rat. "That's enough," said Eugene. "I'll get a newspaper for it."

Eugene went into the kitchen. He thought there were papers from last week on top of the refrigerator, but there weren't. Helen must have used them in packing. He touched the refrigerator and exhaled twice, as deeply as he could. There were newspapers in the darkroom.

Raimundo was down on one knee next to the rat. The pink-bladed knife lay next to his shoe. He had turned the rat over and was tickling its stomach, forcing a reflex scurrying motion from the tiny legs now pointing straight up into the air. A slow thread of scarlet leaked from the rat's mouth to the floor next to its ear. Raimundo made a noise with his tongue, almost a cluck, as though trying to coax a laugh from a baby. One of the rat's front paws slowly clawed the air.

Eugene went into the darkroom. He, too, went down on his knee, but only to pick up the newspapers under the bathtub. He stayed there, staring at the rim of the tub. He had never noticed before what seemed to be sand specks in the white porcelain. There was a chip that looked like the inside of a tiny clamshell. He put his forehead against the porcelain to cool it.

After a moment, he heard running water. He looked in back of him, but no one was at the sink. He picked up the papers and went into the living room. The rat lay still in the middle of the room, all four paws pointed up, its filmed eyes staring, not at the ceiling above, but at the wall directly behind it.

Eugene dropped the newspapers next to it and went into the kitchen. Raimundo was cleaning his knife at the kitchen sink, holding it with the exposed fingers of his left hand and rubbing the thumb and forefinger of his good hand up and down the sides of the blade. Without looking up, he said, "He's dead. I killed him for you." He turned toward Eugene.

"Yeah." Eugene said the word quickly, shortly.

Raimundo went to Eugene, raised the cast, and placed it on his shoulder. The fingers still held the knife, now dripping water. "I did it for you because you are my friend." He took the heavy hand from Eugene's shoulder and went back to the sink.

After rinsing the blade one more time, he turned off the water, then made a move toward a dishtowel hanging on the refrigerator door. Stopping, he looked at the blade, wiped it carefully in slow strokes on his sleeve, examined it closely, breathed on it, wiped it one more time, then folded it back into its handle. Fumbling, he tried to put it into his back left pocket with his right hand, but it fell to the floor, clattering. Eugene wondered if the reverberations would trouble the rat.

Raimundo picked up the knife and tried again, but kept jabbing himself. "You do it for me." He held it out to Eugene. Eugene didn't take it immediately. Raimundo held it out farther. "Here." Eugene accepted it and quickly slid it into Raimundo's back pocket.

"Does it show?"

"A little."

Raimundo shook his hips. "Now does it show?"

"No."

"Good. I don't want Father to see it. He made me promise." Raimundo pulled in a deep breath to celebrate a job well done, and went into the next room.

Without looking at the rat, he went to the table, picked up his wineglass, and drained it. He poured another glassful, sat in the rocker, and began to rock. "That's why he can't live with anyone. Why no one will let him. Why he always has to run away."

"What?" said Eugene.

"That kid. David. Because he is a faggot." He dumped two heaping spoonfuls of sugar into his glass.

12

Eugene burrowed his nose deeper into the pillow until he couldn't breathe any more. Then he withdrew it enough for his right nostril to take in air. The bell clanged again. He started to pull his right arm up so he could put it across the exposed ear, but he felt it crossing flesh. He opened his eyes. Only his right eye could see. The other was lost somewhere down in the pillow. A freckled shoulder and a head of reddish hair loomed up in front of him, with one ear rising from the hair like a pink toadstool. Eugene remembered now. It was Ian.

Ian was an apprentice baker in a German bakery on Eighty-third and Third Avenue. In the bar on Prince Street where they'd met last night, Eugene had detailed and described all the work a combine could do, and Ian, in turn, explained the perils of making a pastry called Mozart kugel.

The bell rang again, and Ian stirred but didn't wake. Eugene closed his eyes and let his arm stay where it was, flopped down over Ian's chest. He realized he had a headache from too much wine. Then he remembered the rat. Slowly drawing his arm back from Ian's chest, he raised himself up so he could see over the sleeping body down onto the floor. There, a white oval about a foot and a half long and one foot wide commemorated the spot where the rat had died. Not content with washing the floor, Eugene had scoured it with cleanser and steel wool, and now it looked as though a spotlight had been locked into focus as an eternal tribute to the rat's tragedy.

Raimundo, when he'd left the night before, didn't even take the rat downstairs with him. Eugene had had to wrap it up and dump it himself on his way out to get drunk. To disown it as much as possible, he put it in a garbage can belonging to a warehouse across the street. Placing the lid back on the can, he hoped—aware that it was a repeated hope that had never yet been fulfilled —he hoped that this time for certain he was ending his involvement with the East Side neighborhood. He would *never* go back. The camera was gone for good, Johnny was dead and buried, and if Raimundo were to come again he simply wouldn't answer the bell. David he wouldn't even think about. Eugene had received nothing he had hoped for from the neighborhood, not the series of pictures, not Johnny, not Raimundo, and he'd lost a camera besides.

The bell clanged again. Eugene lay back and looked

at the ceiling. In the morning light, it stretched neutral and blank from wall to wall like an unpainted canvas. He remembered that he had waked during the night and had stared at it then. It had been no more help then than it was now. It had kept his eyes open but had given him nothing in particular to look at, nothing to distract him from the thoughts and visions that were tumbling through his mind.

There had been a dream just before waking. He had held Raimundo's head between his hands and was banging it as hard as he could against a white stucco wall. A young stranger with a pointy nose and a high forehead stood nearby, watching, not involved. Raimundo's hair bounced forward across his face as Eugene hit the head again and again on the hard white wall. Raimundo's eyes were clenched closed, his mouth open, his jaw locked to resist the pain. Eugene became more aware of the man with the pointy nose. He was the rat. The rat was waiting for Raimundo.

It was then that Eugene had wakened and stared at the ceiling. He was afraid. He had wanted to kill Raimundo because Raimundo had chosen the rat instead of him.

Murder, thought Eugene, jealousy, revenge, all aroused by sex. But was there even more to it than that? As he had lain there in the nighttime dark, there came to him as well his wish from the Saturday procession, that Johnny thrust all his strength, not at the cross, but at him, so that after his orgasm of fury the youth would lie conquered and spent, helpless and defeated. A kind of castration, a kind of death.

Is that what sex contained, concealed? It seemed to him at that moment, staring at the ceiling, that even love itself could be an oversimplified sublimation that spared one a knowledge of its own dark source. It was a diversion, a distraction, from its initial deadly intent.

But he was neither horrified nor disgusted nor guilty; he was overcome instead by a sadness that all this was so. No wonder, he had thought, the sexual sins had been the ones most warned against, the ones most forbidden—but for all the wrong reasons. The guise of sin cloaked the truer crime, and who would be foolish enough not to subscribe to this protection? Who would not prefer to think himself guilty of simple lust when it rescued him from the charge of murder, pride, castration, jealousy, revenge? Who would not rather confess "I had sex with so-and-so" as opposed to "I have murdered my neighbor," "I have castrated my brother," "I have humiliated a stranger," "I have sought vengeance on my friend."

Eugene had turned then in the dark to Ian at his side, a stranger, his brother and his friend. Had he been guilty that night of any of these crimes? Was sexual guilt or sexual sorrow actually a justified reaction to the greater crime, unconsciously committed? Was the act of tenderness, affection, of love even, a necessary exchange of forgiveness?

Again the bell rang out. "McNiven! You got somebody here wants to see you!" It was Mr. DiVoto from the warehouse downstairs. He hated the clanging bell and always yelled up after the third ring. This morning he had been more considerate than usual and had waited for the fourth. The sounds of the truck being loaded thundered into the room, hollow metal drums crashing against each other as they were thrown onto the iron truckbed. Perhaps Mr. DiVoto hated the bell because its sonorities were too civilized in comparison to the clamor of his own creation.

"It's a priest," he called, "and he wants to talk to you about a camera he's got."

Eugene bounded over Ian without touching him and jumped down onto the floor. One foot landed perfectly within the scrubbed oval, and he leaped out, gasping, as though the rat were still there. When he got to the window, he crouched down, sticking just his head out so it wouldn't be seen that he was naked. "I'll be right down."

Father Carusone looked up, squinting behind his black-rimmed glasses. He held up the camera, waving it more in greeting than in triumph. "Never mind. I'll come up."

"No," Eugene begged. "I'll be down in a minute."

"I told him," volunteered Mr. DiVoto, "it was one of your days off." Mr. DiVoto took a malevolent pride in knowing Eugene's full daytime schedule, and whether he was home or not home.

"I've got to talk to you about something," said the priest. "Is the door down here open?"

"If it's after eight o'clock, yes."

"It's after ten."

"It's open."

Eugene watched him go in the downstairs door. He pulled on his khaki pants and a sweater. Ian rolled onto his back, still not waking.

Eugene went to the bed and gave him a slight shake. "Someone's coming up to talk to me. Just stay asleep until he's gone."

"Huh? What?" Ian started to rise sleepily, but Eugene gently forced him back down onto the pillow. "Just stay here until Father leaves. Go back to sleep."

Ian twisted around and looked at him, puzzled. "Father?"

"Just wait here until he's gone."

Maybe it was the hangover or a disorder of the brain itself, or maybe it was the dream about Raimundo and the rat, but Eugene dreaded having the priest in the loft. And not just because Ian was there. Nor was it his habitual unease. This was more like panic. A priest brought with him blessings and grace, and Eugene feared contagion. In his own way, he was no different from those superstitious people who feel contaminated by the evil eye or a hex sign. Just as evil was to them a palpable power, so was good to Eugene. Its simple presence was dangerous, as though grace were a species of the flu. To him, divine possession was far more likely than the demonic variety, and like its infernal counterpart, it could stagger the will and make him helpless.

His night thoughts preyed on him still, prowling,

waiting to pounce. His head throbbed and his tongue was rotting from the dead wine of the night before. What guilts he felt went well beyond his sexuality. Sexuality was incidental, a means rather than an act. It was his means to the act of murder, the act of castration, and if it were denied him, how could the acts be performed without detection?

He heard the priest reach the first landing, then the second. His panic increased. The priest had the power to take his sexuality away. It was the robber at the door, the plundering thief. Almost wobbling where he stood, Eugene waited in the hallway outside the loft for the priest to come up the stairs.

"You're as bad as my parishioners." Starting up the final flight, Father Carusone lumbered along, his large body swaying from side to side in easy rhythm, as if he had enough energy for lateral as well as perpendicular achievement. "None of them lives below the third floor, and most of them prefer the fifth or the sixth." He was smiling, obviously pleased with his mission. For the first time since Eugene had known him, he was wearing a Roman collar and the black serge suit that, in Atlantis, was normal priestly garb.

The camera was slung over his shoulder, swinging happily in its own independent arc.

Perhaps it was the smile, perhaps the sight of the camera, perhaps it was the simple view of the man himself working his way joyfully up the stairs, but before the priest had come halfway, every fear from the moment before evaporated from Eugene's mind, as though he had wakened from yet another frightening dream, curious now and perplexed about what it all meant. His panic was gone. It no longer had any reality, and he remembered it as a distant event that he had barely experienced.

Watching Father Carusone's advance up the stairs now, he felt a quite opposite emotion. A sense of this good man's loneliness, of his isolation, came to Eugene with a sudden force, although nothing in the priest's manner gave either evidence or support to such a notion. Yet there the feeling was, a sympathy for what Eugene perceived as a life where welcomes often had to be earned, where a common humanness had to be asserted, perhaps at the price of dignity or of a native reticence.

That he had considered refusing the priest entrance to his home seemed not only absurd but monstrous, as though Eugene had subscribed to a common conspiracy to keep this man at a distance, to wound him with isolation, to crush him with loneliness. The dream thoughts and the morning panic no longer had any demands, and Ian's presence inside no longer mattered, whatever the potential embarrassment for himself or for Father Carusone, or for Ian, either. For once, nothing must stand in the way of welcome.

"Good morning, Father. Come in." Whatever Eugene's good intentions, his headache rebelled at the attempted enthusiasm, and the greeting seemed to have a slight snarl in it.

The priest strode across the landing and in through the wide-open door. "Sorry I woke you up, but I'm on my way downtown and decided this would be a good time. I had this I wanted to give you, so I thought you wouldn't mind . . ." He stopped. He had seen the mound of blankets on the bed topped by Ian's auburn hair and the toadstool ear. Lowering his voice, he said, "Why didn't you warn me someone was still asleep?"

Eugene jerked his head in the direction of the bed. "My cousin. From Cleveland."

As soon as he had said the words, he regretted them. Not because the sudden movement of his head had sent a hangover throb drumming through his brain, or even because the words were a lie, but because they revealed instantly the effect of the lie, defining for him its essential evil. The words came between himself and the priest, a barrier separating them from each other, and Eugene realized that within the seconds it had taken him to speak them he had, in effect, negated his free and open welcome. He had returned the priest to the isolation from which he had, moments before, been determined to rescue him. And in the process he had removed himself as well. Their true meeting was canceled, and unless they could find some new truth around which to rally, there would come in its place a mere social ritual contrived to conceal its absence. And no one but Eugene would ever know the difference, which made it even more isolating.

He held out his hand for the camera. "Where'd you get it?"

The priest, looking around the loft, lifted the strap

off his shoulder and handed Eugene the camera as though it were no more special than a hat or a coat. His enthusiasm for what he saw seemed to prevent him from answering or even hearing the question. "Quite a place you got yourself here. All this room."

Eugene wasn't sure whether or not this was a rebuke for his having refused to take David in with him, so he decided to let it pass. Turning the camera over in his hands, examining it for new nicks or dents, amazed, even awed, by its excellent condition, Eugene wished he could postpone the rites of gratitude. Not that he wasn't grateful. He was, immensely. But his usual eagerness to develop a roll of film, any film in general and this roll in particular, took precedence. Out of habit, he wanted to make sure it was still intact, that all its pictures could be coaxed immediately into being, confirming his craftsmanship and constructing a solid foundation for his gratitude. He wished the presence of the priest and of Ian, too, might be neutralized for a while so he could, without rudeness, rush into the darkroom and not come out until he and the film had gone through a grappling and overfond reunion.

Eugene opened the camera to check the film. It was still there. It seemed all right. Relieved, he asked, "Would you like some coffee, Father? How about some grapefruit juice?"

"No, thanks. I'm due in court at eleven. Remember? One still in jail from Saturday."

"Oh. I forgot." Eugene wondered if he should ask

to come along. Pictures of the jailed man, or, even better, woman, would be valuable in a series, if one could be put together from what he had on the two films. Remembering, however, that he had film to develop and print, he decided to be satisfied.

"Can we go out in the hall?" asked the priest. "I want to ask you something, and I don't want to wake up your cousin." He started to motion his head sideways in the direction of Ian on the bed, but stopped before the movement was complete. After the suspension of the gesture, he finished the nod, waited the briefest moment, then motioned with his head toward the door to the hallway.

Eugene had seen it at the same moment as the priest. There on the platform at the foot of the mattress was an open jar of vaseline, and next to it a crumpled towel. Eugene's instinct was to go and screw the cover back on the jar, as if that somehow would change everything.

Father Carusone had started toward the door and was looking back to see if Eugene was following. "I won't take more than a minute," he said, no longer whispering or talking in a low voice, as though the vaseline jar had released him from all obligation to be considerate.

Eugene brought the camera with him into the hallway and closed the door behind him. Father Carusone looked up toward the fifth floor and down to the third, listening for the sound of other people. The building was silent except for the resonance of the metal drums on the truck outside and the triumphant cries of Mr. DiVoto following each crash.

Looking directly at Eugene, Father Carusone said, "I've got a favor I want you to do for me."

Eugene returned the look. "Sure. If I can." He prepared an attitude of indifference in case the priest should mention the vaseline.

"Sit down, okay? It might take a little explaining." Father Carusone sat on the top step of the landing. When he didn't continue talking, Eugene sat on the second step of the stairs leading to the floor above. The spindles of the banister between them formed a grillwork, and with each of them facing in an opposite direction, Eugene felt he was in a confessional, but that it was the priest who was about to confess.

Without looking at Eugene, Father Carusone began, "I don't want you to thank me for bringing back the camera. The same goes for the film inside. If I didn't need a favor from you, I would have destroyed them both."

Eugene's curiosity dismissed the indifference he had ready. Apparently the vaseline was not going to be referred to. At least not for the moment. Father Carusone took off his glasses, scrubbed his face with one hand, then put the glasses back on. "You didn't wonder yesterday how I knew your name. Well, I guess you were tired and didn't notice it was a slip on my part. It was on the camera, and your address too. You see, I'm the one who stole it." He paused. "I didn't like the idea of anyone seeing us at . . . well . . . less than our best."

(*177*

Eugene looked at him, but seeing the priest still staring straight ahead as though demanding confessional anonymity, he faced front again.

"You can thank Johnny you got it back. And you can thank whoever stabbed him too. If Johnny hadn't been killed, you would never have got it back. The camera maybe, but definitely not the film."

Now the priest looked up at him through the spokes of the banister. "When you develop the film, if you see who stabbed Johnny, I want you to bring me the picture—"

"But that's no problem."

Father Carusone looked him in the eye, then turned his gaze out again over the stairs leading down. "I want the print you bring me to be the only print, and then I want you to burn the negative, so no one else will ever know."

"But I can't . . ." Eugene turned away before continuing in a lower voice. "I can't do that."

"You don't have to decide right now. Think about it."

"I'm sorry, Father, but if the murder's there, right in the picture—"

"I know," interrupted the priest. "If it's there, you can sell it. Or maybe it'll make you sort of famous."

Eugene was annoyed at having his selfishness and his ambition so easily exposed. He was tempted to be righteous, to put himself on the side of justice, to claim he could never in conscience stand in its path, but he knew Father Carusone could turn such fatuousness against him, humiliate him with it, and then take advantage of his shamed state to force an agreement out of him. The truth, in this instance, was his only refuge.

"All right. Yes. I can probably sell it. And it would mean a lot to me. And I don't mean just the money part of it. So I know right now I won't give it up if it turns out it's there."

Still not looking at Eugene, Father Carusone asked him if he'd ever been in jail. Before Eugene could answer, the priest went on to argue that if the picture was published, the murderer would be put behind bars. And who would that help? Not Johnny, not Johnny's mother, not the murderer, not the Cardinal Archbishop uptown or the Mayor downtown. Nobody. Except maybe some of the other inmates and the guards, because they'd have somebody new to mess up. And maybe the judge, because sentencing a murderer might encourage the illusion he'd earned his paycheck for a change. In his experience, whoever went to jail came out worse than when he went in.

When Eugene mentioned the possibility that the murderer might do it again, Father Carusone said the chances of repeating the crime were greater once he'd been in prison, much greater.

"Then why didn't you just destroy the film? Why'd you bring it here to me?" asked Eugene. He felt inadequate to the decision the priest was asking him to make.

"I can't develop film, and you can. And I could hardly have dropped it off at the corner drugstore." He paused as though reluctant to go on, but continued anyway. "I want to know who did it. I want to know!" There was a yearning in his voice that made Eugene uneasy.

"What're you going to do if you find out?"

Father Carusone looked at Eugene and waited for the moment it took Eugene to turn and look at him. "My reasons, would they influence you one way or the other?"

"I don't know," said Eugene, lowering his eyes, afraid something he might see in the priest, some terrible need, would prompt him to make a promise he might not keep.

Father Carusone turned away. "There's some plaster off the wall down there on the lower landing. I'm going to look at it. I'm not going to look at you. And I don't want you to look at me. Not until I'm finished saying what I'm going to say."

Eugene faced front again and noticed, level with his eye, a small hook screwed into the wainscotting, with no hint of what its original purpose might have been. Looking at it, he could see, only peripherally, the priest on the other side of the spindles that separated them.

"Are you looking at me?" asked Father Carusone. "No."

"It's taken me a while to make up my mind to say these things out loud. Otherwise, I might have offered you the camera and the film when you came around yesterday, or even after Mass on Easter. Anyway, here it is." He hesitated, then began. "First, I'd like to make the

murderer help Johnny's mother if he can, even if it's
something Johnny himself never did." Eugene saw nothing extraordinary about such an idea. The priest went
on. "Then I'd try to comfort him. Because I'm sure he's
suffering too." The priest was beginning to speak with
greater difficulty, as if he were admitting to some
shameful sin. "The murderer must feel abandoned too,
separated from the rest of us. I'd try to remind him . . .
to remind him that there is at least that much of Christ
in him. That feeling of abandonment. That he, that the
murderer, even in his murder, that he shares Christ's
cross with Him."

Eugene could see the huge head shake slowly, as
if the priest were thinking of a truth whose wonder and
sadness he could never accept. "Mercy is so strange. It
lurks in such dark places." The head stopped shaking.
The building was completely still. Even Mr. DiVoto
seemed to have been silenced. Eugene stirred just
enough to creak the step he was sitting on. Father Carusone took the sound as a cue to continue.

"Then I would put my arms around him and I
would remind him that he is my brother." Father
Carusone swallowed audibly. "And I would ask him to
forgive me. To forgive me, because I haven't forgiven
him. And maybe I never will."

He turned and looked at Eugene through the grillwork of the banister. "You can look at me now." What
Eugene saw was the cold and empty eye of a man completely without feeling. An arrogance was set upon the
lips and jaw, too proud to be a sneer, the head itself held

high as if to provide the height necessary for so much disdain and loathing.

Eugene began to raise his hand, not to shield himself from what he saw, but to put it through the spindles, to break through the grillwork separating him from the priest. He wanted to ask him if he, Eugene, could be his brother, if they could embrace and in the embrace feel the weight of each other's burdens for at least that one solitary moment, if they could exchange forgiveness, the two of them between themselves, quick, before God got hold of them with His own terrible brand of mercy.

But a metal drum thundered against the truck below and Eugene saw the priest take off his glasses, scrub his face, then put the glasses back on. The cold arrogance had gone. The old sorrows had returned.

"I can't do it," said Eugene, relieved to hear himself say what he was saying. "I could promise now, but eventually I'd go back on my word. I know I wouldn't burn the negative. I just couldn't."

Father Carusone stood up. "Maybe you'll change your mind."

"I don't think so."

Their eyes met; then both looked quickly away, as if they'd been guilty together of something shameful. Father Carusone put his hand on the banister and took a step down. He reached up and scratched behind his ear, then shook his head as if warding off a fly or a thought. He took another step and stopped. Turning around, he smiled, the same pleased smile he had coming up the stairs. "The reward!" He said it as though it

were the solution to all that troubled him, a solution
that had stubbornly eluded him until that very moment.
"Didn't you say there was a reward?"

Startled, Eugene said, "Oh, the reward." But he,
too, felt grateful at the idea, as if giving money were
at least some form of exchange, and a fairly easy one at
that. The meeting would not be completely futile, after
all. "Sorry. I forgot."

"How much is it?"

Eugene hesitated, loosening his grip on the camera
as if to devalue it. "Twenty dollars?"

Father Carusone puckered his lips up against his
nose. "Is it your food money?"

"No, not really. I mean, not right now, it isn't."

"You got a job?"

"Part-time. A moving company. And sometimes I
do carpentry or I paint apartments. If I really need the
money."

"Then make it fifty."

"Fifty!"

The priest shrugged. "If I'd asked you before you
knew you were getting the camera back, how much
would you have offered? Anything, just to get it back.
So I'll take fifty. In cash."

"What if I don't have that much?"

"You'll get that much."

The questions and the answers, so easily specific,
eased the throb in Eugene's head and helped settle his
stomach. "Okay. Fifty." He opened the door to the loft
and went in. When Father Carusone hesitated on the

landing, Eugene said, "Come in, come in," feeling that the visit was beginning all over again, fresh, with nothing said or done to mar their meeting.

Without saying a word, Father Carusone entered and Eugene closed the door behind him. The priest stood just inside the room, not looking around.

Going to the bed, Eugene tried to lift the edge of the mattress, but couldn't raise it enough to reach the envelope hidden underneath. He looked at Ian, who was still asleep, considered giving him a slight shove to move him away from the middle, but decided not to. He reached his arm under as far as it could go.

Ian shot up in the bed. "What!" He looked wildly around the room.

"I'm only trying to get something from under the mattress," whispered Eugene, as though Father Carusone wouldn't hear.

"Oh," said Ian. "It was you under there. Why didn't you say so?" He flopped down again.

Eugene cried out in pain. Ian sat up again. "What!" Withdrawing the envelope from under the mattress, Eugene squeezed parts of his arm, testing for broken bones.

"You okay?" whispered Ian.

"Go back to sleep," said Eugene, no longer whispering. He took two twenties and a ten from the envelope, made a quick count of what was left, then slid it back under the mattress. Ian slowly raised his head, watched the arm sliding back out, then saw Father Carusone near the door. Bobbing his head in greet .ng, he said, "Hello, Father," then lowered himself back onto the pillow.

Father Carusone put the money into his pocket. "Thanks. It's how much I need to bail the guy out." Looking at Eugene, he said, smiling, "Maybe that's the real reason I brought the camera back. I needed the bail. Bad." He held out his hand and Eugene took it.

Before letting go, Father Carusone said, "You Catholic?"

"Yes," said Eugene. "Yes. I am."

The pressure on Eugene's hand tightened a little, and the priest, shaking it again, nodded his head as if indicating that Eugene had given, from among several possibilities, the proper answer.

Eugene almost blurted out an amendment to his statement of faith, "I mean I *was* Catholic," but he said nothing. What did it matter one way or the other? So much was going on inside his head that both the question and his answer seemed very much beside the point.

When Father Carusone was halfway down to the third-floor landing, Eugene called after him. "Father? If I find out who it was on the film, I *will* burn it."

Without turning around, speaking so low that Eugene wasn't sure he'd heard correctly, the priest said, "No, you won't." He continued down.

"But I will! I'll burn it. I promise I will!"

13

Using the tongs, Eugene agitated the contact sheet in the developing solution, as though trying to shake loose at least one picture that would surface, precise and clear, showing the murder. Or, better, a series on the murder. His pledge to Father Carusone hadn't even lasted until the priest was out the downstairs door. What Eugene wanted now was, first, a picture of the weapon drawn and, possibly, aimed at Johnny. Then the flashing blade the moment before the upthrust into the stomach. Next, the moment itself, the murderer's face, Johnny's face, the clenched fist up against Johnny's side. Finally, the blade withdrawn, Johnny stunned, his eyes amazed, his body tilting slightly downward, falling against someone who will shove him to the ground.

It was only after he had taken the sheet out of the fixer and put it into the wash that Eugene remembered his hangover. At first he thought he was dizzy from watching the contact sheet moving under the disturbed, distorting surface of the fluids. But now, watching the water flow smoothly over the print, he felt not only a dizziness but an uneasiness throughout his whole body, as though his bones were going to dissolve and he would sink to the floor, pawing and twitching, a disorganized hump of cloth and clay that only the most diligent eye would recognize as the remnants of a man.

But the dizziness passed and Eugene was able to examine the prints through the magnifier with a fairly steady hand. He skipped the early pictures of Johnny flogging the cross, went quickly past the singing women and the children; he didn't even pause at the pictures of Raimundo, much less those of David. He wanted to see only the murder. He looked again at all those flailing arms and legs, the contorted faces, the terror and the rage: a man and a woman fiercely clawing each other, an intensification, it seemed, of a tender exchange; a man joyfully smashing a bottle against a lamppost just to be part of the noise and the destruction. One frame was a blur, perhaps a passing stone. Another showed only the diagonal of a thrust arm. One picture, taken from the top step of a stoop, was, Eugene thought, quite perfect. It had a depth of detail drawn forward by the curve of a woman's veil floating behind her as she brought her fists down on the back of a man, who, in falling to all fours, gave the frame a bottom weight to gather and hold the anarchic clamor above. Behind the woman, two men shoved at each other's jaws, while another man had raised his head and eyes heavenward as though calling down a curse on them all. A little girl in the lower left corner was crying and sucking four fingers of her right hand. In the upper right corner, not too near the top, a man stared impassively a little to the left of the camera as though posing for a passport.

The next frame was a blur again, the one after that a man's face, blood flowing down over his eye, his tongue stretched out to his cheek as if he thirsted for his own blood. Then the fat face of a woman who looked as though she were listening very carefully for an answer to an important question. Next, another crowd. Eugene scoured them all for Johnny, for the blade, but neither was to be found anywhere.

Eugene saw Father Carusone's glasses being tipped from his nose; he saw the man who carried the cross waving to someone on the far side of the free-for-all, smiling; he saw Mr. Economu bent double, emerging from a tunnel of bodies as though playing London Bridge. But no Johnny.

Eugene went back and started again with the first frame of the riot. This time he thought he found him in the "quite perfect" picture. He was partly obscured by the woman's veil, but his profile was plain if distant, as was his hand holding a rock aimed at a victim un-seen. Holding the magnifier at various levels, Eugene

---

searched for any sign of the approaching knife, but found nothing. He'd enlarge and print it, anyway.

When he focused the frame in the enlarger, he knew he wouldn't get a perfect print, but even with the slight blurring, there might be enough. As he studied the shadows projected onto the milky paper, isolated now from the full picture surrounding them, Eugene felt something infinitely still come into the room. He coughed on purpose to interrupt whatever it was. The mild bark came and went, but the stillness remained.

Instead of agitating the paper in the developer, he moved it slowly backward and forward, a deeper rhythm than before, a murmur beneath the fluid. Shadows, then clouds began to form, the clouds began to deepen and take a shape, the shape began to define itself, hair, the tip of a nose, the socket for an eye, the line to separate a lip from the cleft of the chin, a sudden splash of black to start the rough surface of a rock, a gathering gray about to become an arm. Other lines began to define themselves, another arm took shape. Eugene could see now that the arm holding the rock did not belong to the slowly materializing face. It was coming toward the face, and there was another arm outstretched to ward it off. More grays emerged as other grays deepened into black. And then the eye was there, the lips were there, the scar beneath the eye was plain to see. It was not Johnny. It was David. The rock was about to be ground into his face.

Eugene yanked the paper out of the fluid and held

it up, dripping. When would the boy stop getting in his way? Would he never be free of him? He let the print plop back into the fluid. It curled over and he had to use the tongs to straighten it out on the bottom of the pan. He wanted to kick the bathtub but remembered he didn't feel well. Of all the intrusions, this was the most enraging. He was convinced that David had thrust himself in front of Johnny while the paper was in the developer. He would never leave Eugene alone.

It would be worthless to print any more of the pictures. They would be David, no matter what the contact sheets had shown before the enlargements were made. It would be David clawing cheeks and shoving jaws. There would be David falling down and David smashing a bottle. David would be crying, four fingers in his mouth, and it would be David posing for his passport.

Eugene doubted that even the Daughters of Jerusalem would survive. David in drag. David being divested of Father Carusone's glasses, David playing London Bridge, and, finally, David—Eugene tried to stop the thought, but it came anyway, roaring through his head: David stabbed. David dead.

Eugene shut his eyes not to see it, but in the dark he saw it all: David, his mouth and eyes wide with amazement as the blade punctured the flesh, the organs underneath emptying, spilling into each other. David bewildered, trying to struggle free of the crowd, David searching for someone, his arms beginning to rise, his palm outward in front of him, David trying to form a word with lips that cannot close, David staring ahead, one hand fumbling along the top of the stretched and soiled T-shirt, David beginning to feel the pain, David being shoved, and shoved again, David struggling to stand, David falling—

Eugene opened his eyes. He looked at the picture. He saw the boy trying to ward off a rock. He saw neither fear nor malice, just David doing his best not to get his skull crushed.

But this simple reality was not enough. Eugene was sick. He had eaten nothing, he hadn't even had coffee. Ian he had sent home without the breakfast he'd promised the night before. Now a chill shuddered through him. He quickly tried to persuade himself that the boy, wherever he was, was in no danger whatsoever. He even struggled to imagine David in some kind of mischief, arguing again with the poor old man in the pawnshop, or stooping to pick up the dime after the funeral, but it did no good. The chill came again, and then again.

Afraid to close his eyes for fear that the vision might return, Eugene looked up at the ceiling as if for help. A fly was walking a jagged crack in the plaster that led from the overhead light to the corner above the mirror. It was like watching a high-wire artist walking on the underside of the wire. The fly continued along the crack and Eugene knew it would tell him what he needed to know. If the fly could make it to the corner, David was safe. The fly stopped. It probed deep into the crack, flitted a little, then moved on. Eugene gripped the rim of the tub and pressed his knees against the side. The boy was going to be all right.

Then, about six inches from its journey's end, the fly flew off to the top of the broken mirror. Eugene let out a quick, open-mouthed gasp as though he had been betrayed. He let go of the tub, stepped back, and watched as the fly feasted on a splash of shaving cream. Then he started out of the darkroom.

At the door he stopped, angrily reminding himself that he was being foolish, that his fears were absurd, even hysterical. He looked down at the print in the developer. If he let it stay there, it would, Eugene knew, continue to darken, blackening completely, until all forms, all shapes were eventually devoured by the dark.

He yanked it out and left the room.

"They didn't turn off the water. The water's still on. They didn't turn it off. The water's not turned off." The repetitions Eugene heard called up the stairway as he stood just inside David's "apartment" seemed necessary so that the whine in which they were spoken could explore all the possible nasalities hinted at in the original complaint. Someone had come into the building, most likely from the basement, since the tin covering on the bathroom window off the fire escape hadn't seemed disturbed when Eugene entered.

He waited for a response to the whine so he could locate whoever else was there, but no one spoke. The complainant, however, offered a second chorus, same as the first. "The water's not turned off. They didn't turn it off. The water's still on."

"Then turn it off." The voice, annoyed but straightforward, called down from the floor above. Too appalled to feel shock, Eugene realized he must have come through the upstairs hallway, past whoever was there, without either of them seeing the other. "I'm busy looking to see what's left behind, so you're the one's got to turn off the water." The voice, a bass, was a good complement to the contralto whine.

Eugene had come back to the neighborhood looking for the boy. He wanted only a glimpse, enough to calm the fears the pictures evoked. He knew that what he had imagined in the darkroom was unreal, that nothing had happened, but still he needed to see him, to catch, if just for a moment, the head again turned slightly to the side, the eyes looking downward, the hair falling forward, shading the scar on his cheek. It seemed a very small thing he wanted, yet until it was done, Eugene knew he would go on feeling this terror that nagged at his heart like a second beat.

"They didn't leave practically nothing." The voice upstairs was surprised and offended.

"I'm not going down that basement turn the water off. All those smoked rats dead right on the mud. Not me. Why somebody, they didn't clean it up? They beginning to stink down there. No, sir. Not me."

"You're wasting time. Turn off the goddam water. We got to get those pipes out before someone else finds

out no one did it yet. Somebody's already helped hisself to the wiring and I don't want this plumbing wasted
like that. Now go on. I'm busy up here."

Eugene preferred not to meet either of them. The
man upstairs was directly overhead now and might be
coming down any minute. He thought he heard the
downstairs man start up. They had come to strip the
place and would hardly appreciate an audience.

Eugene stepped quickly, silently, across the hall into
the charred apartment where the people had died. If the
intruders saw the general ruin, they might pass it by.
A fallen beam and a pile of burned rubble blocked the
door to the farther room. Eugene stepped back into the
shadows of the sleeping alcove and got up onto what had
been the bed. The ashes rose up around his feet soft as
down. The mattress had not smoldered, it had blazed.
He wondered if all the bodies had been removed.

"Don't you come up here. There's nothing for you
up here." The voice seemed muted now, more distant.
The burnt wood, freed by fire of varnish and paint,
absorbed the sound, soaking it into itself like calls
through the winter woods at home.

The sound of steps coming up the stairs drew
closer and Eugene saw a man poke his head in the doorway, look around at the devastation, and pull back. The
steps continued down the hall. He was a short man,
skinny like a rooster, with slicked-back blond hair. The
sleeves of his shirt had been rolled all the way up, as if
to give the appearance of muscle to his arms. He had
a tattoo.

The man met his colleague at the far end of the hall. While the two of them were quarreling, Eugene realized he was pressing something to his chest. Looking down, he saw that he had grabbed David's radio when he heard the plans of the man marauding upstairs.

The quarrel disintegrated into mutterings, and Eugene watched as both men went past the doorway, sullen and discontented. The other was a black man of medium height, who also poked his head into the entrance. He was wearing glasses and carrying a goose-neck lamp. "They sure made a mess in here," he said. His tone was one of appreciation.

"You got to hold the matches while I look for the place to turn it off," said the whiner. "That's all I want you to come down there with me for. You got to hold the matches. That's why. Hold the matches."

"Tomorrow we're coming back and we're bringing the tools. I seen copper up there. Copper running all through this house like it was a mine, the way veins, they run through the ground. Veins. Copper veins like in the mines."

"Hold the matches, that's all you got to do. Hold the matches. Me, I'll do all the work, but I can't work if I'm holding the matches."

"Veins in the ground, that's what they're like. Veins in the mine. The copper mines. Veins in the ground."

The voices retreated down the stairs, the well-matched duet of contralto and bass, each given to its own refrain. When Eugene was sure he couldn't hear them any more, he stepped into the hall and listened again.

There were calls and cries from the street, long and far off, but that was all. In David's room, he put the radio back onto the suitcase and went out quietly. As he was pushing the tin away from the bathroom window, the water in the toilet stopped gurgling.

14

Father Carusone answered the door himself, wearing a pink crepe-paper party hat with silver moons and stars on it. A blue paper napkin was tucked into his belt, and he was chewing. When he saw Eugene, he pulled the napkin from his belt, stopped chewing, and brushed his lips, as though to erase any show of festivity from his face. The hat, however, remained.

"You saw? Okay, I'm ready. Let's have it." He didn't seem all that eager to hear what Eugene would say.

"That's not why I'm here."

The priest almost relaxed. Then he asked, "You mean you didn't develop the film yet?"

"Sure I developed the film, but nothing turned up."

Now Father Carusone did relax. He moved back from the door, relieved, willing now to welcome him. "Good enough," he said. He seemed to consider the film's failure Eugene's virtue. "And thanks for letting me know." He tucked the napkin back into his belt. "Want to come in and have some lunch?"

"No, thanks. I just came to tell you I changed my mind. I mean about David Stokes. He can come live at my place."

Father Carusone looked at Eugene, as though not sure what he was referring to. Then his perplexity faded or, rather, gave way to embarrassment, as if Eugene had just suggested something outlandish and grotesque. Before the priest could say anything, a woman's voice came from down the hall. "Come on, Father, he's going to open it."

The priest glanced back over his shoulder, then looked again at Eugene. His face eased, became neutral, as though he had decided either to forget entirely that Eugene had made such a weird proposal or that it would be taken up at another, more appropriate time, when its absurdities could be pointed out with patience and understanding. "Come have some lunch with us. I made pea soup out of the ham bone from Easter."

"Thanks, no." With effort, Eugene went on. "I want to go find David and let him know what I decided, so he can move in right away."

"Do you really know what you're talking about?" asked the priest.

"He'll have his own room," said Eugene, more defensively than he'd wanted. "The storeroom I fixed up for Helen."

"Helen?"

"A girl who used to stay with me. She moved out Saturday."

"It's a real hotel you're running," said Father Carusone.

"You're not taking me seriously," said Eugene.

The priest shifted his weight from one foot to the other, as though he found himself trapped and wasn't sure which direction, left or right, was the way out. "Sure I take you seriously, but—"

He was interrupted by some words in a foreign tongue, not Spanish, that came from the room down the hall. These were followed by another voice calling, "He's going to open it without you. Come on. Tell whoever it is to come back."

"Come on, please, join us." The priest put his hand on Eugene's shoulder.

"Father, you're going to miss it!" It was the woman again, her warning amused and musical.

"I'll have a few minutes afterwards to talk," the priest said to Eugene, "so come on. There's plenty and we're having sort of a party." He started down the hall toward the room where the voices had come from, his hat with the moons and stars making him look like a harried Merlin whose powers, pale perhaps like the colors of his hat, weren't what they used to be.

"All I wanted," said Eugene, "is to let you know—" His words were drowned out by cheers and applause as Father Carusone went into the room. Eugene turned to go but heard a woman's voice behind him. "Eugene. Come join us, join the party."

Madeleine, the plump, efficient woman he had seen on Saturday, came toward him. She was wearing a light-yellow paper hat, also with silver moons and stars, and had a green paper napkin tucked into the top of her dress. Taking Eugene by the arm, she smiled and whispered conspiratorially, "It's old Father Kincannon's birthday and he's wondering why no one from the old days is here. Please."

She pulled him after her down the hall, a nervous laugh beginning to accelerate so that, when she entered the room with Eugene in tow, she let out a cry of triumph, causing someone at the big round table that filled the room to applaud, as though Eugene were a captured trophy or a surprise birthday present for Father Kincannon. It was Mr. Economu who had clapped and he was smiling now at Eugene, nodding in recognition, his tarnished gold tooth looking like a bad kernel in a row of sweet yellow corn.

"Get him some soup!" said Madeleine. She then whispered into Eugene's ear, "Tell Father Kincannon happy birthday."

The table was crowded and Eugene saw on the far side an old man with hollow, clean-shaven cheeks, wearing a cassock and a Roman collar, slowly lifting with an unsteady hand a spoonful of soup to his lips, unaware, it seemed, that anyone new had joined the party. His hat was blue with silver figures, not stars and moons, but cows and horses, and it was pulled down over his ears like a warm cap for a cold day.

Chairs were scraped and shifted, and a space was opened for Eugene at the table. "Happy birthday, Father . . ." he started.

"Kincannon," whispered Madeleine.

"Kincannon," said Eugene obediently. But he had not forgotten the old priest's name. There were two men at the table besides Father Kincannon, Father Carusone, and Mr. Economu. One, wearing a green hat decorated with the three pigs and the three bears, was a little younger than Eugene himself, a man he'd never seen before. The other was in his late twenties. A bright-orange hat with the seven dwarfs was perched on his straw-colored hair. Father Carusone had mentioned an alcoholic and an ex-seminarian. Eugene's guess was that the pigs and bears belonged to the ex-seminarian, because the man with the seven dwarfs was the alcoholic from the shelter, the one Eugene had given his final Cuprex bath.

A bowl of thick green soup with big pink chunks of ham poking up through it was put on the table in front of Eugene by Father Carusone, and a chair was pushed up behind him. "Bread's right here," said the priest, putting a torn loaf of Italian bread in front of him. "And there's apple pie for birthday cake."

"I'll come back later," Eugene said quietly, trying to edge out from between the chair and the table.

"You think I don't remember you, but I do!" It was the old priest, and he was talking directly to Eugene. "You went to the school."

"No, he didn't go to the school," snarled the seminarian, clearly annoyed at the preposterousness of such an idea.

"He did!" cried the priest. "He went to the school!"

The seminarian opened his mouth to speak, but Father Carusone very matter-of-factly said, "He went to the school," as if to put the subject safely out of everyone's reach.

Mr. Economu, shouting in Rumanian, banged on a brightly wrapped box next to Father Kincannon's bowl.

"Open the present," said Madeleine. "He's going to open the present, everybody!" She tapped her bowl with her spoon, then scooped up a big chunk of ham, picked it off the spoon with her fingers, examined it, and daintily popped it into her mouth as though it were a Fanny Farmer chocolate.

Eugene moved his chair away from the table as quietly as he could. He would literally bow out before too much notice could be taken.

"Used to serve Mass. Altar boy. Served Mother of Perpetual Help Devotions, too!" Holding a spoonful of soup halfway to his lips, the old priest turned to the seminarian and shouted fiercely, as though the younger man were deaf, "Mother of Perpetual Help! You hear me? Mother of Perpetual Help!" He lowered the spoon back into his bowl and glared defiantly at the young man.

The alcoholic was looking at Eugene as if he wasn't quite sure whether they knew each other or not. Eugene felt the dawning was not far off.

"All right, you don't have to shout," said the seminarian to Father Kincannon. "I know what Mother of Perpetual Help Devotions are."

"You don't! Because you're a Lutheran! That's why they kicked you out of the seminary. Because you're a Lutheran!" He turned to Eugene. "Lutheran! Kicked him out! Now you, *you* remember Mother of Perpetual Help." He turned to Madeleine. "*He* knows his Memorare! You can bet your bottom dollar on that."

"You don't say the Memorare at Perpetual Help, Father," she said, examining another chunk of ham, which seemed to meet with her approval. She plunked it into her mouth.

"Open your present, Father," said Father Carusone, gently touching the freckled back of the old priest's hand.

"I was not kicked out. I left," said the young man. "And even if I *were* Lutheran, so what?"

"Go on," Father Kincannon said, waving his spoon at Eugene like a flag to which he was being asked to rally. "Recite it. Show these heretics and infidels what a real prayer sounds like. Go on, don't be afraid. *I'm* here."

The old man's pale blue eyes flared as he leaned toward Eugene, but there was no anger in them. There was instead a fear he had seen before in people like his grandfather, a terror that something precious was about to be taken from them, that someone they loved was about to leave them, perhaps forever. " 'Remember, O most gracious Virgin Mary.' Say it!" Father Kincannon banged the table with his fist.

Eugene turned to Father Carusone. "I just wanted to let you know so you could take care of it with Mrs. Stokes if . . ." He felt the alcoholic across the table staring at him. As he looked over, the man leaned back in his chair, his blue paper napkin half crumpled in his hand. His eyes narrowed with suspicion, then widened with recall. A slow smile stole across his lips. He looked Eugene up and down, not, it seemed, to reinforce his memory, but to make a mocking appraisal of his body. His smile stretched to a leer, and he folded his hands on his lap, very amused at what he remembered.

Eugene wanted to turn and run, but he felt a claim was being made on his courage, and not the last he could expect. He sat down and, ignoring the alcoholic, spoke to Father Carusone in as low and conversational a tone as the frog in his throat would allow. "I don't want to go see his mother if I don't absolutely have to, for her sake as much as for mine, in case that Mr. Zalensky is hanging around. So if you'll just let her know David's with me and that it's all right."

" 'Remember, O most gracious Virgin Mary,' " growled the old priest at Eugene from across the table.

Father Carusone folded his paper napkin next to his bowl and sighed a long sigh. "Cut it out, will you?" It was not a dismissal but a plea. "David can't live with you. You know that."

"Yesterday you thought it was a great idea," said Eugene, not taking his eyes from the priest.

"I know I did. But now . . ." Father Carusone scratched at the napkin, then went on in a low but annoyed voice. "That wasn't quite your cousin from Cleveland this morning."

The man from the shelter was listening carefully, still leering, obviously enjoying more than anything Eugene's discomfort.

"Okay," said Eugene to the priest, "you're worried and I don't blame you. So am I. But one of the things I came here to tell you was not to worry. Nothing's going to happen. If it does, I . . . I'll give up the whole thing." He tried to clear his throat, but had to continue with the rasp still in his voice. "You've got my word for that." Eugene thought he heard the man from the shelter snort.

" ' That never was it known!' Say it! You remember it! The Memorare!" yelled the old man. Mr. Economu applauded the excitement with his puffy hands, laughing, then rapidly tapping the top of the box with a single finger, like a woodpecker.

"Look," said Father Carusone to Eugene, "be sensible. Why put yourself into an impossible situation? It's no good for anyone."

"I just came from that tenement I told you about, where he's living. Two guys were going through it, getting ready to strip out the plumbing. But they didn't have their tools. It's not David without water scares me.

What if he'd been there when they came in, or if he's there when they come back tomorrow? Anybody can get in if he wants to, and who knows what could happen? David's not going to stay there. He's going to come live with me for now."

"He'll stay here then," said Father Carusone, flatly, wearily. "With us. We'll find room."

"He won't stay and we both know it. How many places did you say he ran away from? No matter what you do, he'll be back in that burned-up place before the next day. But me, he'll stay with me. I know he will. He won't run away." Eugene struggled again to clear his throat, but without success. He went on; some of the words he had to whisper. "And he'll . . . he'll be all right."

"I just can't see it," said the priest. "For your own sake, suppose something goes wrong? The kid gets confused, tells everyone what happened, then where are you?"

"What do I have to do to convince you nothing's going to happen?"

" 'That anyone who fled to thy protection, implored . . . implored . . . fled to thy protection, implored . . .' " The old priest sputtered, his lips trembling.

" 'Implored thy aid,' " said the seminarian, exasperated.

" 'Implored thy aid,' " continued Father Kincannon, " 'and sought . . . and sought . . .' "

Eugene, who'd been looking only at Father Carusone, felt a bony hand clutch his arm just above the wrist. The old priest was looking at him, pleading. " 'Sought thy . . .' "

" 'Intercession,' " said Eugene quietly.

" 'Intercession,' " said the priest, nodding. "Yes, yes. Then what?"

" 'Was left unaided,' " said Eugene in a whisper.

"There!" cried the priest. "I told you! Served Perpetual Help!" He clutched Eugene's arm even more firmly. "And then what? Then what happens? Tell them!"

" 'Inspired . . .' " said Eugene. He stopped and looked at Father Carusone for help, not because he'd forgotten the prayer, but because he didn't want to say the words in front of all these people, especially the man from the shelter.

"Tell them what happens next," pleaded the old priest, as though Eugene alone could pronounce the words that would rescue him from unspeakable peril.

" 'Inspired by this . . .' " said Eugene softly, but the seminarian took over, rattling out the words, impatient to get it all over and done with. " 'Inspired by this confidence, we fly to thee, O Virgin of Virgins, our mother.' "

"Yes . . . yes," breathed the old priest, indifferent now as to where his rescue might come from. He began to smile. Eugene looked down at the table. "Then," asked Father Kincannon, "then what happens?" Eugene tried to withdraw his arm, but the old man held on that much harder.

Madeleine patted the old priest's cheek and spoke

as though telling him he was the best-behaved and most loved little boy on the block. " 'To thee we come, before thee we stand, sinful and sorrowful.' "

"Yes?" said the priest longingly, not looking at her, still grasping Eugene's arm.

Madeleine stopped patting his cheek and tucked the old priest's napkin under his Roman collar as she continued, chattering casually, as though cheerfully repeating neighborhood gossip. " 'O Mother of the Word Incarnate, despise not our petitions, but in thy mercy hear and answer them. Amen.' "

Father Kincannon withdrew his hand and pounded the table. "I told you he knew it! Went to the school! Anybody went to the school knows it." He glared at the seminarian. "And remembers it!"

"*I* went to the school," cried the seminarian, hurt and frightened, as though his patrimony were being taken from him.

In low tones, Father Carusone said to Eugene, "If your mind's all made up about David, what'd you come tell me about it for? No one's really got to go to Mrs. Stokes. She doesn't care one way or the other, so long as he's not there with her and Zalensky."

"I'm here," said Eugene, trying to speak quietly enough so the alcoholic wouldn't hear, "because I'm not going to make it a secret like I was doing something wrong. I want his mother to know and his teachers at school to know. And I want you to know."

"What am I supposed to tell them, his mother and the teachers?"

"Tell them he's with me, with . . . with someone who's going to take care of him sort of, someone who . . . who'll make sure he's safe and he gets the right things to eat, and he's safe and . . ."

"Safe?" asked Father Carusone sadly.

"Yes," said Eugene. He cleared his throat. "Safe." He cleared his throat again. "If you don't want to get involved, if you really want me to go see his mother myself . . ." He stopped, hoping the priest would speak. Father Carusone said nothing.

The man from the shelter was shaking his head from side to side, still smiling.

Eugene pushed his chair back and stood up.

"Your soup!" said Madeleine. "And he didn't open the present yet! Here, take my hat." Reaching over, she crushed the yellow crepe-paper hat down onto Eugene's head. "And," she continued, "you didn't tell us about your camera, if you found it or not." Breaking off a piece of the bread, she put it next to Eugene's bowl. "When I think of what happened to our beautiful procession . . ."

"Procession?" said Father Kincannon. He had begun to undo the ribbon on the package, but stopped. Father Carusone closed his eyes to protect himself from what he knew was about to happen, then opened them and looked wonderingly at Madeleine, as if asking why on earth she had brought *that* up.

After swallowing a spoonful of soup, Madeleine said, "Sorry." Then, slapping the box, she turned to Father Kincannon. "Open. Open."

The old priest glared at Father Carusone, who was staring down into his empty soup bowl, resigned, waiting. Father Kincannon took in a long, deep breath and let it out in one explosive shout. "Procession!? A massacre, that's what it was!" He pounded on the box, making a tear in the wrapping and denting the cardboard.

"You want some help opening it?" asked Madeleine sweetly. She reached toward the box, but Father Kincannon thrust her hand aside. "Crucifixion right out in the streets! What are we in? The Middle Ages?"

"Some of us are," said the seminarian, blithely examining the ceiling.

Father Kincannon ignored the remark and leaned across the box toward Father Carusone. "Well, it won't happen again, I can promise you that. Don't think I haven't been in touch with His Eminence, the Cardinal Archbishop himself, because I have. And he feels the same way I do. There'll be no more crucifixions, take my word for it!" His hands, trembling as much with anger as with age, began twisting the ribbon on the box, tugging at it with all his strength. "No more crucifixions, not in this neighborhood! Not next year. Not ever!" The ribbon snapped.

"He's opening it, everybody, he's opening it," Madeleine mumbled through the piece of bread she had stuffed into her mouth. The man from the shelter continued to look at Eugene, the leer now fixed onto his face. The ex-seminarian stopped slurping his soup, and Mr. Economu began beating time on the table with his hands, providing a ceremonial tattoo for the opening of the birthday box.

Father Carusone was still looking down into his empty bowl. He didn't move. "I'll fix it with David's mother," he said quietly. "But I have your promise. Remember that." Raising his head as if he'd just finished saying grace, and with the abrupt good cheer that announces the end of solemnities and the beginning of festivities, he said to Father Kincannon, "It was Madeleine's idea, but Mr. Economu picked it out."

Mr. Economu applauded the mention of his name.

The seminarian put his spoon down to watch that much more closely Father Kincannon's difficulties with the wrapping. Eugene backed toward the door. The man from the shelter winked at him and pretended he was trying to suppress his leer.

Closing the outside door behind him, Eugene heard old Father Kincannon calling out, "No more crucifixions! Not next year, not the year after! Not ever!"

On the sidewalk outside, the wind rustled the crepe paper, reminding Eugene he was still wearing the yellow hat with the silver moons and stars.

15

Vacant lots are never vacant. Eugene sat on a plastic Dairylea milk crate and looked around him. He saw the beginnings of next year's Golgotha, no matter what old Father Kincannon and the Cardinal Archbishop had decreed. A mattress, probably ridden with bedbugs, was hunched against the wall of the building at the back. A tin kitchen cabinet, its door kicked in, its top drawer open, was lying on its side like a dog that had been run over. The obligatory abandoned car had not yet been delivered, but one tire and a part of the motor had already arrived, along with a front seat. There was a small mound of half-burned garbage, dampened by coffee grounds that had not yet dried. The eggshells had been grayed in smoky wisps like Easter eggs dyed for someone who was color-blind anyway. Stones and broken bricks

were strewn everywhere, and in a clump of grass beginning to turn green, someone had constructed a small
rock pyramid about a foot and a half high. Whether art
or altar, or only a heap of stones and bricks, Eugene had
no idea, nor had he the energy to even wonder.

He was eating a small blueberry pie and drinking
the Coke he'd bought in the A&P across the street. He
hoped the food and drink would, if not cure his hangover, at least give ballast to his stomach, which had been,
all through his interview with Father Carusone, a free-
floating object. The sight of the green-pea soup with
those pink chunks of ham hadn't helped. After the pie,
he planned to eat an apple, and if that didn't work, he
would revert to an old childhood remedy, a Hershey
bar with almonds.

What he really needed more than food or restored
good health was some rite of exorcism that would ban-
ish from his mind the man from the shelter. It worried
Eugene not at all that the man might tell Father Carusone about the incident after the Cuprex bath. That
would tell the priest nothing he didn't already know.
What haunted Eugene was the leering grin, its smug
assurance that Eugene would fail at what he wanted to
do. It was as though he were being watched, even now,
by some malevolent power that knew all it had to do
was wait patiently and the whole enterprise would
collapse with a devastation that would be general for
everyone involved. It was so sure of itself. What frightened Eugene was that he might already have entered into
a pact with it, given it a secret promise that what it

was waiting for would sooner or later be delivered by Eugene himself, an obscene offering in its honor.

Still, he had to look for the boy. He had to find him. He had no choice.

He folded the pie wrapper neatly so it would fit easily in his jacket pocket. The Coke bottle he put on the peak of the rock pile. Feeling unwell made him fastidious. He wiped his mouth on his sleeve and imagined he felt better, until he stubbed his toe on a venetian blind laid across his path. The rattle of the slats seemed to create a responding rattle in his bones, leaving him all but unsupported except by the habit of walking upright.

Standing on the pedestrian overpass that separated the park from the housing project, Eugene looked down along the strand of trees and grass. The bushes along the walks were fully leaved and the buds on the sycamores seemed aching to unfurl. A large clump of forsythia sprayed its golden shower behind home plate of the baseball diamond. The grass was already strong and green. The dismal Easter rain had helped.

Eugene looked down the length of the park. Two little girls were solemnly playing catch between the pitcher's mound and first base. Beyond them on a long green field, a full-dress soccer match was in progress for the benefit of about twenty spectators. One team wore wide-striped gold and black jerseys, the other green and brown, each team looking like a different breed of bumblebee.

Beyond the soccer field, Eugene saw the trees where David had waited on Easter morning. Nothing stirred. Near the river the green metal barrel that had been meant to hold the Easter fire had been knocked over on its side like a defeated rook in a game of chess. Along the paved path that ran at the river's edge, people strolled, one man jogged, and a pack of dogs yapped after a bicycle.

Across the water, Brooklyn was brilliant in the afternoon sun, and the river itself seemed serene in spite of a tug, a sightseeing boat, a white-sailed sloop, and a motorboat all plowing its surface, countering its currents.

Down in the park, Eugene went first to the river and looked out over the water, as though this were somehow the river's due, a greeting owed, an obeisance required by the local god, a ritual to be performed before any other business could begin.

He went next to the green barrel and set it upright, another debt whose origins he couldn't quite remember. Someone had made the necessary holes along the bottom to ventilate a fire. Inside, some wood was half burned.

Eugene started down the river path toward the far end of the park. He paused to watch the soccer match long enough to consider, one by one, each of the spectators. David was not among them. Where the path strayed slightly to the right, leading into a small thicket of trees and bushes, Eugene followed, looking up at the trees, down into the bushes, and ahead along the path, as though the boy might again be hiding.

Standing at the back of the park amphitheater, he felt himself waiting, hushed, for the entrance of the audience as well as the actors. No one came.

He stopped at the end of the park and looked through the chain-link fence onto the paved lot filled with parked trucks, then reversed direction and went back along the river.

By now, evening was on its way, the sky had begun to cloud over in the east, and the air was beginning to chill. Going to the railing, he looked down at the water. Green before, now it was black even on the surface. Its ripples had grown to waves that seemed to be hurrying upstream, away from the harbor, as though they had to be home before dark. Across the water, Brooklyn had turned gray as if with age. The park was beginning to empty. Sounds carried a greater distance, drawn out longer by an evening sadness.

He looked once more down the length of the park. The soccer players were straggling toward the overpass. A rust-colored dog was nosing the playground slide. Eugene went to the barrel and looked inside. He dropped in his pie wrapper and watched it float down to the ashes at the bottom. After it settled, he went to a trash basket and tugged out a torn shopping bag. He brought it back to the barrel, crumpled it, and shoved it down under the wood, then waited until the paper expanded into a shape more comfortable to itself.

He walked through the grass and collected twigs, going all the way down to the clump of trees. Looking into the darkening grove where the ground was strewn with broken sticks and fallen branches, he hesitated, then entered.

When he stooped to pick up a twig, the smell of the damp, cooling earth rose to his nostrils with a steamy sweetness, almost of deepest summer. He dropped the twig and slowly stood up. He felt he was in a grove of elderberry and boxwood at the far side of his grandparents' cow pond. He was a boy of six and he and his grandmother were picking berries. High in a distant tree a crow called in a coarse whine, sounding like a telegraph wire relaying news of some recent calamity. He heard his grandmother praise the plenty of that year's yield and predict a special flavor for the wine she always made. The earth was soothing and cool on his bare feet. He looked down at the berries in his pail and counted six strung in a small arc at the bottom rim. They looked like a red caterpillar.

Overhead, a white summer cloud crossed the sun, and in the sudden shadow a secret knowledge was given to him. He was an exile on the earth. His grandparents' home, when he would return that evening, he would know to be a house of secret beauty and secret sorrow, and this knowledge would make him forever a stranger in its rooms. And this secret, it was revealed to him, he would take with him into the great world, where, too, he would be an exile, and this burden would never be lifted from him for as long as he lived.

The white cloud passed and the leaves were suddenly projected again onto the ground at his feet, as though heaven itself had set its seal, irrevocable and beyond appeal, on what had passed.

He heard his grandmother's laugh as she pulled the berries from the bush and sent them raining down into the pail on her arm. The sweet smell of the earth steamed up into his nostrils, but he could not look at his grandmother, because he knew his heart would break for pity and for love.

Eugene leaned down again, picked up the twig, and took his kindling back to the barrel.

When the flames rose high, he stared through them, back toward the trees. Nothing moved. He traced with his eyes the circle where the worshippers had stood, then looked again through the flames. He saw no one.

Eugene watched and waited until the trees turned into a black cloud at the end of the dark field. He looked down into the fire, the flames hot on his face, the light flickering against his eyes. He watched the wood burn until the largest board, placed at a diagonal against the wall of the barrel, collapsed and sank down into the fire, sending up a flare of flames and a puff of sparks and ashes.

He loved the boy. With all the yearning of his exile, he loved him. The secret beauty, the secret sorrow had again been revealed to him, and if he had tried all those times not to see the boy, not to see the flopping hair, the akimbo ears, the worm-scarred cheek, it was because he had felt, as on that distant day, that his heart would break for pity and for love. Now he *had* to take him in, no matter what.

On the overpass, Eugene looked back one final time. The fire still burned. Two men, one a green and the other a golden bumblebee, were gazing down into the barrel, as if to affirm their wonder that this indeed was a true and honest fire.

16

Eugene heard the music from the stolen radio and started down the dark stairs from the silent bathroom, feeling his way along the wall. The hallway had warmed since the afternoon, and the smell of smoke was touched now with a sweetness that Eugene knew was working itself up from the asphyxiated rats in the basement. The rough plaster on the wall sanded his fingertips as he continued down, step by step.

He saw candlelight flickering faintly through the doorway to David's apartment and was about to call when he heard a voice in a near whisper say, "Don't move. I'll tell you when to move." The words coming from the room were not spoken as a warning or a threat but an instruction. Eugene went to the doorway and looked in. Someone was coming d rectly toward him from the shadows on the opposite side of the room, emerging from among the long streaks staining the wall. When the someone didn't take a second step, Eugene saw that it was his reflection in the smoked mirror above the mantel. It seemed to him his own ghost, terrified at seeing him intrude into territory where danger waited.

"You're moving. Don't move. Not yet. I'll tell you when to move."

Both Eugene and the ghost surveyed the room to see where the words came from.

"Almost. Not yet. Don't move." A trace of warning had come into the voice, and the half whisper was a little hoarse. The tempo of speech had increased.

Eugene stared into the recess of the alcove, where the light of a single candle was sending massive shadows up the wall. What was first a stirring now became the heaving of a solid form as it rose and fell on the bed. Seeing it, Eugene could now hear a repeated thud that quickened to a slap, the sound of flesh on flesh.

"Don't move. Don't move." The warning had become a plea.

It was Raimundo. Eugene could see the sweating face begin to contort as the youth thrust himself down, drew himself up, then thrust himself down, again and again. The sharp slaps had the sound of a whip, as though it were Raimundo again, in agony, punishing himself again against the back of Christ.

"Not yet. Not yet. Don't . . . Don't . . . move . . ."
There was a sound of tears far back in the voice, and
a strangling of mucus in the throat.

Eugene caught a quick glimpse of the ghost in the
mirror rearing back as if threatened with a vision it
could not bear to see. Then the ghost vanished and it
was Raimundo Eugene saw. He had not heard him
jump up from the bed, nor had he seen him come from
the alcove. He was standing in front of Eugene, panting
and sweating.

"Ahh! It's my friend." Raimundo, relieved, reached
out the arm with the cast and laid it on Eugene's
shoulder, the same sign of friendship he had given after
he'd killed the rat. He withdrew the arm and pulled up
the other side of his pants, his erection disappearing
inside but still lunging against the line of his left pocket.
He didn't zip his fly or hook the clasp at the top, but
held his pants closed with his good hand. "Why didn't
you tell me you come here too? I thought I am your
friend?"

David was sitting on the edge of the bed, his pants
down around his shoes, his arms resting across his knees.
Most of his shirt was still bunched up onto his chest. He
stared down at the floor as if trying to identify it, to
place it in the context of floors he had known.

Eugene spoke to him calmly. "Pull up your pants.
Let's go." David didn't move. Eugene went and stood in
front of him. "Come on. We're going."

Raimundo touched Eugene lightly on the arm.

"Wait. I'm not through yet. I thought it was a junkie and I had to stop to be ready for him if it was. Now I can go finish."

Eugene looked down at the boy. "You ready to leave?"

"You don't have to go," said Raimundo. "You can do it here. I'm leaving soon as I am finished, if you don't want anybody else around. Johnny, he would never let anyone else be here. We would tell him it was because he didn't want us to see he liked it. He would get mad, oh, would he get mad."

Eugene reached over and pulled David's T-shirt down to cover his chest. David didn't resist, nor did he help. He just sat there. Eugene got the shirt down far enough to cover part of the boy's back.

Raimundo tapped Eugene on the shoulder. Eugene kept trying to pull the shirt down. "You didn't come here to do it to him?" asked Raimundo.

Eugene kept tugging at the shirt. "No."

"Yes, you did." Raimundo stepped back, as though that would give him a clearer picture of what Eugene was doing.

"Sit up straight so I can fix your shirt." David looked up at Eugene, then slowly lowered his head without changing his posture.

"Oh yes you did. You came here to do it, the same as I did. I am not the only one. You do it to him too!"

Without turning to look at Raimundo, Eugene said quietly, "No, I don't."

"Oh yes you do. You do it now. I am not the only one. Everyone, he does it. You do it too, not just me." There was fear in his voice, and desperation too.

"Sit up straight." Eugene jerked at the shirt.

"You are going to do it and I am going to see you do it."

Eugene turned and saw Raimundo tuck in his shirt and fasten his belt. "I am not going to be the only one, like I am a faggot."

"No one thinks you're a faggot."

"I am not a faggot. I only do it because I have a woman. If I didn't have any woman, I wouldn't have to do it."

"I know." Eugene turned again toward David, but Raimundo continued. "And now you are going to do it, and I am going to see you do it."

Eugene heard the click of the blade. David looked up, then pulled his shirt down by himself.

Eugene turned toward Raimundo. The knife was poised as it had been for the rat, only now there was, on Raimundo's face, a look of pleading, as though he were begging Eugene's help.

"It wouldn't prove what you want it to prove if I did it," said Eugene. "It's what I do all the time. So what does it prove to make me do it?"

Raimundo began to lower the knife, but abruptly raised it again. "You're saying that because you don't want to do it."

"Yes. I do."

"No, you don't. But you will anyway! Like I did it." His grip on the knife tightened.

"What if I can't?"

"Think of your woman."

"I don't have a woman."

"Think of your woman, I said!"

Eugene felt a tug at his pants leg. "It's all right," David said quietly.

"See?" cried Raimundo. "He wants you to. Now do it!"

Eugene looked beyond Raimundo toward the tinned windows at the far end of the room and wondered what could be seen now in the smoke-webbed mirror. Perhaps his ghost was grinning now, a bitter, mocking leer.

"No," said Eugene as matter-of-factly as he could, "I'm not going to do it."

Raimundo spoke very carefully to make sure Eugene understood. "You are going to do it. I did it. Now you are going to do it."

David slid farther back onto the bed, still sitting up. "It doesn't matter," he said.

Raimundo took a step closer to Eugene and pointed the knife toward his neck. "You are my friend," he said, sad as always.

"No, I'm not your friend," said Eugene. "You were a friend, to me you were. But I only wanted to make use of you. The way you use him. I'm sorry."

Raimundo shook his head, rejecting the entire

thought before it could even get near him. "Don't talk. I don't want to hear any more talk. Now, are you going to do it?"

Eugene opened his mouth and for a moment his lips didn't move. Then, not knowing what he was going to say, he heard the word "No."

Raimundo looked at him, their eyes met. Suddenly he shoved Eugene out of his way, and by the time Eugene had steadied himself, Raimundo had flung David face-down on the bed. He jerked the boy's shirt back up to his shoulders and tugged the pants down below his knees. Putting the tip of the blade between the buttocks, angled for entry, he looked over at Eugene.

David's hands slowly reached up above his head. He tried to grip the edge of the mattress, but he was too far down on the bed.

"Are you going to do it," said Raimundo, "or am I?"

As Eugene came to the bed, he heard David whisper into the musty rug that covered the mattress. "The door. Is it locked?" Eugene did not remind him there was no door.

One of the Daughters of Jerusalem, her mouth opened to a scream, had turned aside to escape a stone, revealing the body as it began to fall. The blade was in Johnny's side, now being withdrawn. Eugene went back three prints, four, looking for Raimundo, the knife in his hand. He knew he was the murderer.

In the red glow of the safelight, he examined through the magnifier all the enlargements he'd just made, the tangled bodies looking now as though they were struggling against an engulfing wave. He could hear the shouts, but they sounded, in the darkroom hush, like cries of the drowning, calling out for rescue. It was as though the Red Sea had closed too soon upon the chosen of the Lord, dashing them against each other in a tumult of divine making. No longer were they beating and pummeling each other, but were instead reaching out, one to the other, as to a savior. Eugene almost thought he saw himself among them, his arm raised high, one with them at last, crying out lest he perish. But he didn't pause. He continued to look for Raimundo. "You are my friend," Raimundo had plaintively said when leaving the burned-out apartment. But it was revenge that Eugene wanted now.

He had had to shake the boy unmercifully to convince him afterwards that he was to come and live with him in the loft. When he'd gone to Father Carusone, he was determined to be dignified and calm, but after the first few words, he began to sputter and to choke. It didn't stop him. He told the priest that he had failed and that he didn't give a damn that he had failed. Maybe he would even fail again, but still he'd keep the boy. Father Carusone had given him brandy to drink and he had drunk it down in a single gulp. He had spit out the words that he wouldn't give up just because he was imperfect or unworthy.

"Fuck unworthy! Who *is* worthy? Who is?"

(2 2 7

To prevent the tears when they started, he'd gouged his knuckles deep into his eyes. He'd slammed the door behind him when he left.

On the third print, in a background blur, Eugene found the blade and followed it along the arm to the face. It was partly hidden by the fist of the man who had carried the cross. Eugene saw what could be coarse brown hair splayed out over the forehead like a displaced cowlick. He saw the wide nose and the well-proportioned lips. The shirt, unironed, was open at the throat. It was himself he saw.

Three times Eugene slowly raised and slowly lowered the magnifier, the figure losing substance, paling into nothingness each time he raised the glass, but waiting for him there, unmoved and unmoving, when he lowered it again.

Eugene traced once more along the arm and saw the clutched knife and Johnny straightening to receive the blow. Slowly he traced his way back again. And there again he saw the face shaded by the shock of hair. He kept staring at it.

He could not have taken his own picture. No one else could have taken it. There was no film left in the camera when he'd put it in the pouch. And, besides, this picture came not at the end of the roll but earlier on.

He looked again: the hair, the same open-throated shirt he was wearing now, all a gathering of shadows emerging from the chaos of the chosen people desperate not to drown.

His mind, he told himself, had gone. He was still

drunk from the night before, or from the brandy the priest had given him. He had damaged his eyes when he gouged at them. He could not be seeing what he saw.

Gripping the magnifier as if it were the last solid hold on his sanity, he beat back one more attack of nausea.

The bell clanged and clanged again. It was David letting him know he'd collected all his clothes from Daniel's as he'd been told, that he'd arrived for good.

Little by little, Eugene relaxed his grip. He heard the boy's steps coming closer on the stairs, trudging painfully, the suitcase he was dragging bumping against the wall. Looking down at his own blurred and insubstantial self, he ceased to care whether what he saw was there or was not there, a fevered trick or an immutable accusation. He put the magnifier aside. He accepted what his eyes had seen.

Then he lit a match. He had promised Father Carusone he would give him the single print of the killer if he found him, then burn the negative. He would keep only part of the promise. He touched the match to the print. The priest would never see it. No one would. Only he, Eugene.

In the light of a blue and pale gold flame, the blade, the arm, Johnny, the man who had carried the cross, the tangled bodies crying out for rescue, the shadowed face of Eugene himself, all slowly melted as the burning print hunched itself into a crinkled husk of glistening black, like the shed skin of some shining creature of the dark.

The negative, when Eugene burned it, sizzled and sputtered like frying fat and left behind on the top of the tub a crisp shriveled ridge that looked like a burnt worm.

He heard the door to the loft open, then close. "I'm here!" the boy called.